new World, new Horizon

(Screenplay Novel)

Jawaharlal Shanmugam

INDIA • SINGAPORE • MALAYSIA

ISBN 979-8-88749-899-7

DEDICATION

I dedicate this book to:

* Young talented Indians keen to take this country to greater heights in its growth and development.

* Aged parents who are facing many challenges in their lives.

* Persons with disabilities, caregivers, and Institutions doing yeomen service to bring about inclusiveness in society.

* All healthcare workers and support services who are engaged in fighting the Covid -19 pandemic.

* Our farmers who are toiling so much to provide food.

ACKNOWLEDGEMENT

* Sincere thanks to my family, relatives, and friends for their support and cooperation in my endeavour

* I value the relationship of my schoolmates, collegemates, and former colleagues.

* I am indebted to my wife, Sujata Verma, for her constant motivation and encouragement to finish the scripting of the novel.

* My gratitude to Mrs.Sharda for her valuable insights and the mandala artwork on the Prologue page.

* I appreciate Mrs.Sonia Sunny Thomas for participating in the first version of the project.

* My sincere thanks to the Notion Press team – Madumitha M S, Shiny Grace, and Kushagra Kumar for bringing out the novel's publication.

NOTE FROM THE AUTHOR

This novel is presented in a partial screenplay format and written for a specific screen time of 2 hours duration. As such, each chapter will have the depiction of scenes and the activities in that scene. The scene heading will convey the place of action, the time of the day, and the interior or exterior activities. The novel is not an exact screenplay, and as such, there is no transition element from one scene to another. The final shooting script will get altered.

To some extent the author has used his corporate and personal experiences to bring in subtle and sublime elements in the story telling process. Any reader from a college level can easily understand and assimilate the story related to the current trends in the country.

The first version of this story in screenplay format, is registered with the South Indian Film Writers Association, vide Registration No.1680 dated 13/9/2006. Reproduction of the current manuscript in any form without the consent of the author is strictly prohibited.

PROLOGUE

NATARAJAN: Boy's name is Mahesh. Well qualified – B.Tech., M.B.A from a premier institution.

Now, Radha slowly takes the small piece of chapati to her mouth but doesn't utter a word.

NATARAJAN: Mahesh is working as a Regional Manager for the famous multinational FMCG - Joe & Shan Ltd.

Radha takes another small piece and dips it into the vegetable kurma dish. Then, she eats slowly. Seetha is seriously preparing chapati in the kitchen. She wants to serve them hot.

NATARAJAN: Mahesh has Sevvai dhosham too. As such, his horoscope matches yours perfectly.

Radha becomes furious now. She looks at her father angrily.

CHAPTER 1

SCENE 1: EXTERIOR, BESANT NAGAR BEACH ROAD – EARLY MORNING

8th May, 2018 – 5:45 AM

Cutting through the streaky diffusion of early morning light through the heavily wooded avenue, a female majestically drives a Toyota Fortuner SUV smoothly. Few females would handle this beauty in the country as this luxury SUV is predominantly a male's pride. Well, this proud female driver is different and unique in many ways. Why not! The SUV gently halts in the designated parking bay of the famous Elliot's Beach Road. The early morning beach walkers casually seated on the parapet wall see this gorgeous damsel parking her vehicle. She is the cynosure of all eyes.

SCENE 2: EXTERIOR, BESANT NAGAR BEACH – MORNING

Beaming with tremendous confidence, Radha, a tall, well-structured female in her late twenties, comes out of the SUV. Wearing an Adidas trendy turquoise blue Bermudas with a matching light blue striped T-shirt and an equally matching sneaker, Radha is grace personified. In her attire, Radha looks like she is the brand ambassador for Adidas. Sporting her coolers, she admires many boys playing Frisbee on one side of the shore. Radha gracefully walks inside the beach towards the sea, admiring many activities along the way. There is a group playing beach volleyball. The players stop and watch the charming Radha walking by for a moment. They feel rejuvenated, and their spirit seems sky high.

The golden twilight hue on the horizon looks majestic over the sea. As Radha strolls gently, there is a voice from her back.

"Hi! I am Radha. Coming to this wonderful beach early morning is my daily routine. My day starts with seeking the blessings of the almighty sun and water. To me, the five elements of nature, which we call Pancha Bhootham, represents true God. I am not a very religious or a highly spiritual person. To be candid, I don't know the true meaning of these terminologies. Well, I see God within me through my wonderful organs and outside me through the beauty and power of mother nature. God is omnipresent and omnipotent. Friends, this is my personal belief. Don't mistake me or perceive me as if I am an atheist! Simply put, I am not. I go to temples to meditate and have peace of mind. I firmly believe that there is some power in holy and sacred places. For that matter, I go to holy places of other religions too. You may think I am a secular person. Yes, I am. To me, religion means humanity. That sounds like a simple definition! Whether you agree with my philosophy or not is not my botheration. You believe in what your mind says. Better to keep life simple and cool to go forward."

Radha comes close to the sea. The gentle waves keep caressing the beach in a rhythmic fashion and harmony. Nearby, the fishermen are hauling the net vivaciously to see the priced catch for the day. Radha is eagerly watching their excitement. Next, Radha goes near a small unoccupied fibre boat. Sitting on the boat's bow (front part), she removes her sneakers, tugs the socks inside, and gently drenches her feet into the water. Then, carrying the sneakers in her right hand, she loves walking on the wet sandy beach with the waves stroking her feet softly. Walking on the damp sand gives a good feeling to the feet as if we are walking on the microcellular rubber surface.

After doing two laps on the long wet sandy stretch, Radha returns to the same boat to dust her feet. Again, sitting on the bow, she takes a soft dusting brush from her mini shoulder sling bag and gently removes the wet sand sticking to her feet. She allows her feet to dry. In the meantime, Radha takes her mobile and looks at the messages she has received. Her smiling face radiates some happiness through what she has perused. Well, she spends 10 to 15 minutes of the morning looking into WhatsApp messages. Scanning them is like a stress buster. Wearing her sneakers again, Radha smoothly strides on the shore towards the parking bay.

A small popular kiosk on the pedestrian walkway abutting the road serves traditional South Indian unique cuisines using spices, herbs, and medicinal plants. Radha orders a glass of soup and a mouth-watering sweet rice variety (Puttu). The vendor gives her the dishes with a sweet smile, and it looks like the vendor knows Radha too well as she is a regular customer. Sitting on the small parapet wall with her legs stretched, Radha relishes. Chucking the waste into the Corporation dustbin meticulously, Radha waves her hand toward the vendor and proceeds to her SUV. Then, gracefully and stylishly, she drives the vehicle away from the beach road.

The day has just begun for Radha, and she has many things to catch up on in her hectic schedule.

CHAPTER 2

SCENE 3: EXTERIOR, RIVER VIEW APARTMENT – MORNING

Overlooking the beautiful Adyar River, the apartment is one of the posh, well-known residential buildings in the locality. A typical high-end four-bedroom flat with three balconies. The apartment has a good view of the famous Theosophical Society and the Bay of Bengal. The ground plus six storeyed building has just twelve flats with stilt parking. This building has modern amenities, including a gym, games room for billiards and Table Tennis, an indoor swimming pool, and a community theatre. If someone has to own a flat in this building, definitely the person has to have a unique stature. Radha's Fortuner SUV stands majestic inside a stilt parking bay, reflecting the brand image.

SCENE 4: INTERIOR, RIVER VIEW APARTMENT, RADHA'S FLAT – MORNING

Natarajan, Radha's father, a retired General Manager from a nationalised bank, is sitting in the hall reading the newspaper. His wife, Seetha, a pious-looking lady, comes into the hall with the lunch bag. On a big table is a beautiful statue of Lord Ganesh, decorated with flowers. Radha comes from her bedroom into the hall gorgeously dressed in dark blue pants and a matching light blue half sleeve shirt. Holding her laptop bag, she is geared up and looking charged. Natarajan closes the paper and gets up cheerfully.

SEETHA: Radha, I have kept Sweet Pongal, Ven Pongal and Vadai for you and Kishore.

RADHA: Oh! So sweet of you, ma. My boss loves your preparation.

Natarajan goes near Ganesha's idol and takes the small silver tray having two cups filled with sacred ash and kumkum. He shows it to Radha. With respect and devotion, Radha takes a pinch and applies it to her forehead. Next, Seetha pins a small bunch of jasmine flowers onto Radha's tresses. The ash, kumkum, and jasmine flowers give Radha an enhanced beauty typical of a traditional Tamil female. Seetha hands over the lunch bag to her smilingly.

Natarajan and Seetha accompany Radha to the main door and proceed to the elevator. Natarajan and Seetha are standing close to her, admiring their wonderful daughter leaving for work. The elevator has come to the floor. Before entering, Radha sees her parents affectionately.

RADHA: Bye, pa. Bye, ma.

Natarajan being a spiritually and religious-oriented person, reciprocates humbly. Waving his hand,

NATARAJAN: Radhe Krishna, Radhe Krishna.

Seetha waves her hand too. Radha enters the elevator. Natarajan stands still like a rock and keeps looking at the elevator door.

SEETHA: Come, let's get in.

Both of them get into the hall and take a seat.

NATARAJAN (emotionally): I don't know when God will open his eyes to our Radha!

SEETHA: Did God not open his eyes and give beautiful gifts to our daughter! Humm! B. Tech, Gold medallist from IIT Madras. M.S from the University of California. Senior General Manager in a major MNC IT company. Handsome six-figure salary with two houses! She drives a Toyota Fortuner! Moreover, she looks charming. What more do you need in life?

NATARAJAN: Yes. True. God has given all those beautiful gifts. I don't deny it. All these means nothing if she is single. She has to settle with a good person. Getting a groom for her looks extremely difficult with her stature and the Sevvai dhosham (Manglik dhosham) she has in her horoscope.

SEETHA: God will show her the ideal groom. Don't worry.

NATARAJAN (emotionally): Seetha, before I close my eyes, I want to see a wonderful Krishna for our Radha. I want to have Radha on my lap in the marriage hall and see the groom tie the Mangalsuthra to her neck. That's enough for me. I'll be blessed if God can give me that one golden opportunity to cherish in my life. After that, God can take me away.

SEETHA: Have faith in God. It will happen.

NATARAJAN (tearfully): I don't know how long I will be alive! I know my days are getting numbered. I am eagerly waiting for the Lord to call me. Not able to take the torture.

Seetha is looking at her husband sorrowfully.

NATARAJAN: On one side, my cancer is killing me. On the other hand, my daughter is not getting a groom because of

Sevvai dhosham. It is killing me differently! It is worse than cancer.

SEETHA: For heaven's sake, please do not open the Sevvai dhosham topic with her. She will get agitated. She becomes furious hearing those two words. For Radha, they are like demons to her.

NATARAJAN: Seetha, from the groom's side, rejection is happening just because of this defect! They are feeling scared of marrying her! Even in modern times, people follow all these traditional things in our community. It is just crazy. What sin did we do to have our daughter born with a Sevvai dhosham?

SEETHA: Don't let your mind get worked up. It will spoil your health further. Come, have breakfast. Leave it to God. He has big plans for her. We don't know. Put the burden on Lord Ganesha. He will take care. Poor girl, she sacrificed a great career in the US only to be with us. Let her be happy here.

Seetha brings a delicate balance and composure in handling the situation as a loving mother and a wife with enormous maturity. She acts like a vital bridge between a sinking husband and a modern, highly educated daughter caught in a tight situation of traditional religious beliefs, customs, and practices.

SCENE 5: EXTERIOR, IT CORRIDOR HIGHWAY – MORNING

Radha, wearing her trendy coolers, is waiting for the signal to turn green. She has to take a left turn to enter the pride of Chennai, the famous Information Technology Corridor Highway, otherwise known as IT Corridor Highway, to the Chennaites. From other vehicles, people are gently glancing at Radha. The glance gives a feeling that she must be in a good position in one of the IT companies in the corridor. Her demeanour is enough to convey the subtle message of her socio-economic status. Radha is also conscious that people are watching her. In a way, that's a sign of admiration for what she has accomplished. Radha knows she has many more miles to go in her life.

As the green light flashes, Radha stylishly takes a left turn and gracefully drives. Slowly, we hear her voice in the background.

"Driving this road is like driving to heaven. This road is an inspiration for thousands of people who look for greener pastures in their life. Many believe this road is the future gateway to prosperity and has transformed many people's lives. This road is undoubtedly the pride possession of Chennai and India. Before 20 years, this road was nothing, but today, it has everything. That's the beauty of a transforming India."

Many vehicles are zipping the broad lanes to start their day with renewed hopes.

SCENE 6: EXTERIOR/INTERIOR, RAMANUJAM IT PARK – MORNING

Radha takes a U-turn of the IT highway signal and comes and stops in front of the big gate of the sprawling Ramanujam IT Park. She is waiting to go through the security corridor. The barrier rod opens for her SUV to pass through. The security person operating the entry point salutes her with a gentle smile. Radha reciprocates. Once again, there is her background voice as she goes towards the designated parking building.

"**Well, this is my Indraloka.** Coming into the campus, I have eternal bliss. I am fortunate to work inside this iconic

building, named after the great mathematician of the world –
Ramanujam. It is a fitting tribute the Government of Tamil
Nadu has bestowed to one of its greatest sons of the soil.
Ramanujam is my big inspiration to excel."

*Radha parks her SUV on the first floor and proceeds to the
elevator.*

CHAPTER 3

SCENE 7: INTERIOR, HIGH TECH GLOBAL HEALTHCARE SOLUTIONS – MORNING

Radha gracefully keeps her index finger to the scanning machine at the entrance door. Her profile appears on the small monitor screen. With a gentle smile, she registers her entry into the office. The glass door opens for her to make her way into the broad aisle slowly. In many cubicles, intelligent girls and boys in their early and mid-twenties harmoniously work on the computer system. As Radha walks by, her colleagues greet her. She reciprocates. Radha sees one of her colleagues seriously working with apt attention on the computer screen and having her two palms on her chin. Radha slowly goes behind her. Keeping her right hand on her shoulder,

RADHA: Sunitha!

Sunitha gently turns back and sees Radha without winking her eyes.

SUNITHA: Good morning, ma'am.

RADHA: Good morning, Sunitha. Just relax. Take it easy.

SUNITHA: Thank you, ma'am.

RADHA: At 11 am, we'll have our team's meeting in the mini-conference room. Okay.

SUNITHA Okay, ma'am.

RADHA: Cheers

Radha shows a thumbs-up sign to her. Slowly she walks past the individual cabins meant for senior managers. She stops in front of a cabin with a name board reading S. KISHORE (Director – Projects). Kishore is Radha's immediate boss. She gently taps the door and opens it. Smilingly, standing near the entrance,

RADHA: Good morning!

KISHORE: Hi! Good morning.

RADHA: Amma has prepared Sweet Pongal, Ven Pongal, and Vadai. She was particular that I should hand it over to you.

KISHORE: Oh! So sweet of her. She has lovely hands. She makes delicious food.

RADHA: How about having coffee?

KISHORE: Sure, give me 15 minutes. I'll send this mail.

RADHA: Okay.

Radha shows a thumbs-up sign to her boss and leaves the cabin. The name board of the adjacent room reads RADHA NATARAJAN (Senior General Manager, Projects). Gently, Radha inserts the key and opens her cabin door. A beautiful, well-furnished 20 feet by 15 feet room look elegant. A medium-sized six-inch sandalwood Ganesha statue is on a glass tray. Before occupying her seat, she prays silently for a few seconds and then touches the idol with her right hand to seek his blessings. Then, taking a few rose flowers from her handbag, Radha decorates the Lord Ganesha. This small spiritual act is her daily ritual before the commencement of her work.

SCENE 8: INTERIOR, HIGH TECH GLOBAL HEALTHCARE SOLUTIONS, CAFETERIA – MORNING

Radha and Kishore have occupied a circular corner table, and both seem to relish the typical Madras filer coffee. Later, biting a coconut cookie, Kishore looks at Radha.

KISHORE: Radha, in the coming days, we expect a prestigious project from MNC Jackson Pharma and Life Sciences, New Jersey, USA. They want to focus on the Asia-Pacific region.

RADHA: That's good news!

KISHORE: We are trying to strike a total package with them.

RADHA: Brilliant.

KISHORE: You know! They were highly impressed with the inventory management, ordering, and tracking software we have created for other companies.

RADHA: We can tailor make to suit their specific needs. We can create many trends and analyses incorporating statistical models for their Management Information System (MIS). We can create good data analytics.

KISHORE: Absolutely.

RADHA: I firmly believe that any software we design should help the management improve their efficiency and effectiveness.

KISHORE: True.

Kishore has another sip of coffee and looks at her.

KISHORE: Radha, we may have to visit New Jersey next month for a week to finalise the project.

RADHA: Cool. Looking forward to the visit.

KISHORE: Radha, mark my word, the management is highly impressed with your work. You are like a darling in the organisation.

RADHA: Kishore, you know me well. I give my best to anything I undertake. You have been my pillar of support in many ways.

KISHORE: Take it from me; you have a great future. I'm counting on you for this project.

RADHA: Sure, Kishore. Just leave it to me. Relax.

KISHORE: The management is keen to give you a free hand. You decide what you want and the way to go about it. We are here to support you.

RADHA: Cool. That's enough.

KISHORE: Radha, you are more than a colleague to me. I feel rejuvenated when I interact with you. You always give me positive vibes. I only wish I have you as my life partner.

Radha gently keeps her right hand on his left hand.

RADHA: Me, as your life partner! Is it possible? Humm!

Kishore looks at her and has a sip.

KISHORE: Something is coming our way as a stumbling block. You know it well.

RADHA: Both of us know. I don't know If it is a curse on me. But, Kishore, to be honest, the issue is killing me.

KISHORE: Okay, let's forget the topic. Come.

It looks like Radha and Kishore like each other. They look like a perfect couple – a made for each other pair. But something is coming in their way as a significant impediment. What is the issue?

SCENE 9: INTERIOR, HIGH TECH GLOBAL HEALTHCARE SOLUTIONS, CONFERENCE ROOM – MORNING

Radha is seriously discussing with her team of seven project managers, working on a big hospital information system project for a leading chain of hospitals. Sunitha, the Group Manager, is making the presentation standing before them.

RADHA: Sunitha, when can we finish the complete digitising of patient records.

SUNITHA: Ma'am, one-month maximum. I am putting another three members to the hospitals for this assignment.

Pramodh, another team member, echoes his views.

PRAMODH: Ma'am, the scanner at two Pearl Hospitals broke down. They said either they would get it repaired or buy a new one. Once they install, we can finish it fast.

Stephen, another dynamic member, shares his views.

STEPHEN: Ma'am, my team is working to integrate laboratory and imaging services with the wards. Doctors and staff nurses can easily access reports in their system. We are also incorporating strict security access.

RADHA: Fantastic. When can we see the demo?

STEPHEN: By next week, it should be ready.

RADHA: Great.

Radha sees Roshan.

RADHA: Roshan, how about integrating Pharmacy and Surgical stores with the wards?

ROSHAN: Ma'am, we are working on the idea you gave us. The doctors and nurses can get much information regarding the availability, fundamental pharmacological aspects, and substitutes. A noteworthy feature is that we have created a unique product coding system.

RADHA: The search for the desired product should use the therapeutic index in multiple ways. Okay! For example, we can search Gelusil through the alphabetical index, alimentary system or antacids. I presume your coding design considers these, I guess.

ROSHAN: Absolutely, ma'am. Two digits represent each classification in the eight digits product code. We have four classifications.

Radha looks at Ismail, another vibrant and brilliant system analyst and designer.

RADHA: Ismail, you are working on inventory management and ordering.

ISMAIL: Design is coming out well, ma'am. We have incorporated 3 and 7 days of moving average trends for sales figures.

RADHA: Discuss with the General Manager, Purchase and Pharmacy, regarding ordering quantity levels. Your formula should give flexibility for the quantity they want to hold as an inventory. The consumption of infusion items like Glucose, Dextrose, and Sodium Chloride solutions is in large volumes. They occupy ample space in the stores. The Pharmacy can have four or seven days of stock because it is readily available with the distributors. Critical antibiotics need to maintain a good inventory for at least 15 to 21 days or more. You can't have a uniform formula across the board. Do you get my point?

ISMAIL: Yes. Ma'am. We discussed this with them. In the ordering module, we have five variables of stock inventory. 4, 7, 15, 21, and 28 days. The ordering person can decide.

RADHA: I guess the formula considers the opening stock for the month, purchases made, the correlation with the current closing stock, the average sales, and the moving average trends.

ISMAIL: Yes, ma'am.

Radha sees Sunitha.

RADHA: Sunitha, we will visit the main Pearl Hospital. We will have a meeting with the senior management people. Our good friends there will also feel happy.

SUNITHA: Sure, ma'am.

RADHA: Okay, buddies. We will meet on Friday at 3:00 pm. I hope we will be finalising many aspects. Director Kishore is keen to have an overview of the user-friendly software that we are creating. He highly appreciates the data analytics we have incorporated into the modules. Prepare well. Any issues/ clarification, knock me down anytime. Okay! Keep motivating your team members. Let me tell you, this project's success will springboard many good things. Keep that in mind. Right! Cheers to all of you.

Radha and her team leave the conference room smilingly. All of them seem to be happy and cheerful.

SCENE 10: INTERIOR, HIGH TECH GLOBAL HEALTHCARE SOLUTIONS – AFTERNOON

It is 4:30 pm. Inside the cabin, Radha is seriously packing her bag. It looks like she is calling it a day a bit early. She usually stays until 6:30 or 7:00 pm. Then, Radha locks her cabin door and sees Sunitha.

RADHA: Sunitha, I have some urgent work. Call me in the evening after 9 pm. Cheers, baby.

SUNITHA: Okay, ma'am.

Radha knocks on the door of Kishore and gently gets in. Kishore looks up.

RADHA: Kishore, the Oncologist, called me. Going to the hospital to meet him.

KISHORE: Why? Anything of concern!

RADHA: I don't know. He must have got the Pet Scan report of my father. I am keeping my fingers crossed.

KISHORE: Need any help; call me.

RADHA: Sure, buddy. After meeting the Oncologist, going to Holy & Sacred Home to take tuition for five plus two students. Next week, they have exams.

KISHORE: You are doing a great job, Radha. I salute you.

RADHA: Kishore, we must give something back to our community and society. Otherwise, we will not have any meaning in our life.

KISHORE: Absolutely. Okay, carry on. Take care.

Radha shows her thumbs-up sign and smilingly departs.

CHAPTER 4

SCENE 11: EXTERIOR, GANDHI NAGAR 4TH MAIN ROAD, ADYAR – EVENING

Radha drives the SUV into the quiet road leading to her apartment building. There is hardly any vehicle, and a middle-aged couple wearing traditional dresses walks along the pedestrian pathway. Radha slows her car towards the couple and lowers the left window. Then, smilingly, she looks at the couple.

RADHA: Rajan Uncle, good evening. Shall I drop both of you?

RAJAN: Oh! Radha, good evening. Thank you, ma. We will walk down. In a way, a good exercise for us.

RADHA: Okay, uncle.

RAJAN (blissfully): Radha, here. Have temple prasadham.

Rajan extends his hands through the window.

RADHA: Uncle, wait. I'll come out and receive.

Radha stops her engine and comes out, giving due respect to the couple. Even though Radha is highly educated and modern, she knows how to carry herself in different situations. She takes the sacred ash and kumkum from Rajan and applies them to her forehead. Rajan's wife, Shanthi, gives her a small garland. Radha bows to it with reverence and pins it to her tresses. Looking at the couple,

RADHA: Uncle, I have forwarded your son's CV to my HR department. I will try to fix him up somehow. Don't worry.

RAJAN: Radha, you will be doing a great favour to my family.

RADHA: Tell Aswin to call me. Next week, I'll fix up the interview for him.

Shanthi steps forward. She catches Radha's hands emotionally.

SHANTHI: Radha, you have a big heart for helping others. God will shower enormous blessings on you.

After the small meet, Radha gracefully drives her SUV. Rajan and Shanthi keep admiring the vehicle going.

RAJAN: Shanthi, God has given her beautiful gifts, but the supreme forces have still not shown an ideal life partner. Her parents are so worried.

SHANTHI: The Gods have big plans for her. Through God's grace, Radha has achieved many good things in her life.

SCENE 12: INTERIOR, RIVER VIEW APARTMENT, RADHA'S FLAT, BEDROOM – EVENING

Radha is coming out of the bathroom wearing a dark green below-the-knee cotton skirt and a nice loose light green shirt matching it. She towels her hair to dry. It looks like she has freshened up after a hectic day's work. Her mobile phone rings. She sees the caller as Kishore.

RADHA: Hi! Kishore.

Radha gives a patient listening but somehow looks a bit dull in her outlook.

RADHA: Kishore, the report is not good. The Doctor has clearly said a maximum of one year of survival chance. Cancer has spread to the intestine and lungs. 4th stage metastatic cancer!

Radha becomes emotional and has a few drops of tears dripping down her cheek. From the other side, Kishore seems to be comforting her. (Intercut with Kishore). Kishore is relaxing on the balcony of his house.

KISHORE: Are you going to reveal the status?

RADHA: No, Kishore. I'm not going to open up with my parents. Why disturb their peace and happiness? They don't know that I have met the Oncologist.

KISHORE: Yeah, better to maintain silence. I'll offer my sincere prayers to the Gods for your father's peaceful life.

RADHA: Thank you, Kishore. Appreciate it. I'll catch up later.

As she is towelling her hair, there is a knocking sound on the door. Radha gently opens the door and sees her mother.

SEETHA: Radha, Appa is waiting for you to have dinner.

RADHA: Amma, give me five minutes.

SEETHA: Fine. Today, I've prepared stuffed chapati and mixed veg kurma.

RADHA: Fantastic, ma. My mouth is watering.

Radha catches her mother's hands and gives them a gentle kiss. She looks at her.

RADHA: Amma, my boss, Kishore, liked your Pongal and Vada.

SEETHA: Dear, my job is to make you happy and cheerful. Okay, I'll organise dinner for you people. Come fast. Don't be on the phone.

Seetha leaves blissfully.

SCENE 13: INTERIOR, RIVER VIEW APARTMENT, RADHA'S FLAT, DINING HALL – EVENING

Radha and her father, Natarajan, are seated perpendicular to each other. Seetha is serving them stuffed chapatis and accompaniments. Slowly Natarajan sees Radha curiously.

NATARAJAN: Radha, today we have received a good alliance and a matching horoscope.

Radha listening to her father, stops eating and sees the plate. She has a small piece in her right hand but is not in the mood to take it to her mouth. Instead, she gently sees her father without winking her eyes. Natarajan is keen to open it out and feels this is the right time to catch her attention.

NATARAJAN: Boy's name is Mahesh. Well qualified – B.Tech., M.B.A from a premier institution.

Now, Radha slowly takes the small piece of chapati to her mouth but doesn't utter a word.

NATARAJAN: Mahesh is working as a Regional Manager for the famous multinational FMCG – Joe & Shan Ltd.

Radha takes another small piece and dips it into the vegetable kurma dish. Then, she eats slowly. Seetha is seriously preparing chapati in the kitchen. She wants to serve them hot.

NATARAJAN: Mahesh has Sevvai dhosham too. As such, his horoscope matches yours perfectly.

Radha becomes furious now. She looks at her father angrily.

RADHA: Appa, never bring the topic of Sevvai dhosham and horoscope. I get wild when I listen to these words. They are like deadly demons to me.

Seetha is disturbed by the increasing decibel level of Radha. She senses some hot discussion is going on with them.

NATARAJAN: Radha, we may not show importance to these things, but the groom's side is very particular even in this modern world.

RADHA: Appa, I am not interested in marital relationships based on that stupid and irrational horoscope matching. To me, that paper is horror scope. This Sevvai dhosham is killing me. It is worse than metastatic cancer. Please, Appa! I beg you with folded hands. Just leave me alone. Please.

Seetha is coming with a plate containing hot stuffed chapatis.

NATARAJAN: Okay, Radha. As you wish, I'll stop talking about your marriage henceforth. Happy!

With tears dripping from his eyes, Natarajan gently wipes with his hand towel. He looks at Radha sorrowfully. Seetha is thoroughly disturbed and sees her husband.

SEETHA: Why do you discuss marriage issues when she has food?

NATARAJAN: Seetha, I'm counting my days. I know my cancer is spreading fast. I would like to see my daughter marry before I close my eyes.

Radha, in a disturbing manner, gets up. She has left half chapati on the plate. Then, with tears, she goes to the wash area and rinses her mouth.

SEETHA: Radha, please have. I have specially prepared. You have left it on the plate. What did the food do to show your anger? Radha, it is Annapoorini ma.

Radha doesn't heed her request. She is crying. The words of her father touched her emotionally. She cannot sit in front of him and visualise the disturbances that he is going through. In a way, she knows the ground reality that her father may survive a maximum of a year. However, she cannot digest her marriage based on the horoscope matching. Her Sevvai dhosham is like a deadly curse fallen on her. Silently, she wipes her face with a hand towel and proceeds to her room. Seetha is remorseful and looks at her hubby.

SEETHA: Look, when you talk about her marriage, peace gets disturbed in the family. I have told you umpteen times not to broach the subject. You don't listen.

NATARAJAN: Looks like I've gone mad. (*After a pause*) When a person knows he will die soon, his mind doesn't work correctly. I think I made a big mistake opening the topic with her. (*Catching her hands sorrowfully*) Seetha, I'm sorry.

He looks at Seetha emotionally.

NATARAJAN: Seetha, go and comfort her. Like an idiot, I spoiled her mood.

Seetha gently puts her hand on his shoulder to comfort him first.

SEETHA: I know your inner feelings. You know Radha loves you to the core. I'll take care of her. Finish your dinner and relax.

SCENE 14: INTERIOR, RIVER VIEW APARTMENT, RADHA'S FLAT, BEDROOM – EVENING

Radha is lying diagonally on her bed in a prone position with her face tucked into the pillow. Seetha slowly sneaks in with a plate in her hand. Placing it on the beautiful rosewood table, Seetha gently sits near Radha and puts her hand on Radha's head.

SEETHA: Radha, get up. Look at me.

Radha is slowly crying. Seetha pats. She takes Radha's head and slowly places it on her lap. This act is a true reflection of motherly affection to soothe her daughter's feelings. Radha hugs her mother and weeps profusely now.

SEETHA: Hey Radha! You are a highly mature, cheerful, and brave girl. Get up. You are not a child to cry like this.

Radha soberly looks at her mother.

RADHA: I wounded Appa today.

SEETHA: Radha, your father has a responsibility to see you settle. He is keen to see you getting married before he passes away. That's his only wish. Is there anything wrong with his thoughts? He just brought to your attention a prospective groom. That's it. Accepting or rejecting the proposal is in your hands only.

RADHA: Amma, I'm not interested in marriage. You know the reason.

SEETHA: Look, Radha. One day you need to settle in your life. Okay, you decide whom you want to marry. Settle with any boy from any religion. No issues. Your happiness is our happiness.

RADHA: Amma, I don't want to marry anyone based on that horoscope paper. I'm very clear about it. I need to find the right man.

SEETHA: Fair enough. Then you pick your man. As parents, we are only requesting you to look at Mahesh. Who knows! He might be a good person for you. Just interact with him like a friend and see. There is no compulsion that you should settle down with him. You can reject the proposal if you don't like it. We will accept any decision of yours, ma. Happy!

Radha feels a bit relieved. Seetha feeds Radha the chapati as how a mother would give a tiny tot. At last, the tender motherly touch has provided the needed solace to the daughter.

CHAPTER 5

SCENE 15: EXTERIOR, RIVER VIEW APARTMENT, PARKING – MORNING

Radha, elegantly dressed in light blue jeans and a matching orange shirt, gracefully opens the door of her SUV. She places her laptop bag and the lunch bag that her beautiful mother has given her. With Madurai jasmine flowers tucked into her plaited hair, her face radiates that of a white lotus about to blossom brilliantly with the luminescence of the morning sunlight. This lotus is unique, an epitome of courage, knowledge, and wisdom to unleash new waves to enhance life's quality, meaning, and purpose. Wearing the trendy and stylish Ray-ban coolers, Radha gently enters the SUV with grace and style personified. She drives out of the gated community with the security person at the main gate, giving her a royal salute send-off.

SCENE 16: EXTERIOR, GANDHI NAGAR 4TH MAIN ROAD, ADYAR – MORNING

As Radha drives her SUV, she sees her father coming piously in the opposite direction, wearing the traditional white dhoti and shirt. Radha slows down her vehicle and stops. Coming out of her vehicle in a remorseful way, she removes her coolers and waits for her father. Radha has tears flowing on her cheek and gently wipes it. Undoubtedly, the last evening's incident disturbed her a lot. Natarajan sees his daughter and slowly comes near her. He shows his right palm having the Ganesh temple's sacred ash (vibhuti) and kumkum with tears flowing. Radha, with reverence and respect, applies it to her forehead. Then, sadly, she sees her father.

RADHA: Appa, extremely sorry…. I apologise.

Natarajan is stunned and sees her apologetic facial expression but doesn't say a word. He also knows he has hurt his wonderful daughter and wounded her feelings badly.

RADHA: Appa, I wounded you. Sorry, pa. I'll not do it again. I promise.

Slowly, she falls onto his chest. He hugs her gently and pats her.

NATARAJAN: Dear, you have not wounded me at all. Why should you apologise? I think I made a colossal blunder.

Knowing the union and conversation are on the road, Radha comes out of his clutches and holds his hands.

NATARAJAN: Radha, I have taken a owe before Lord Ganesh. Henceforth, I'll not open my mouth about your marriage.

(He becomes emotional)

NATARAJAN: No, dear. I don't want to see my ever-smiling and beautiful radiating daughter getting wounded. Your happiness is my happiness. I know Lord Ganesh will show you a wonderful person one day. I have immense faith in him. He will make it happen. Okay, go to the office with your lovely smile. No tears, dear.

Radha heeding his request, wipes her tears.

RADHA: Appa, I love you. I want to be with you and amma. What I am today is because of my beautiful parents. I am blessed and gifted. Okay, pa. I'll get going.

Natarajan opens the door for Radha to enter. He knows that the more he is involved in the conversation with Radha, the more she will become emotional. But, on the other hand, he doesn't want to spoil her mood as it would impact her work. Radha sees her father through the door window and shows her right hand. Natarajan gives a gentle kiss on her palm.

NATARAJAN: Go, dear. Have a wonderful day. Call me when you reach the office. Okay! I want to hear your sweet voice till my last breath. That happiness is enough for me. Go, ma.

RADHA: Okay, pa. I love you.

Seeing her father emotionally and tearfully, Radha raises the window and gently drives away. Natarajan keeps admiring his adorable daughter. Now, he becomes expressive and not able to control his true feelings. He cries. This expression genuinely reflects a father's impeccable love and affection towards his daughter. Wiping his eyes, he turns back and strolls towards his apartment.

SCENE 17: INTERIOR, HIGH TECH GLOBAL HEALTHCARE SOLUTIONS – MORNING

Radha slowly and stylishly walks through the broad corridor in the vast hall leading to her cabin. Enroute, many of her colleagues greet her, and she reciprocates softly. Opening the door, she offers her morning customary silent prayers to Lord Ganesh's idol on her table. She takes her seat and portrays a sorrowful face, picks up her mobile and dials it.

RADHA (softly): Appa, reached office. Once again, sorry. I was rude to you yesterday. I know you'll understand my feelings.

Radha has tears flowing down and wipes. Inwardly, she knows her father's countdown to his longevity has begun. She is going to see him for a few more days only. After his demise, there will be a big vacuum in her life. From the other side, Natarajan reciprocates the call.

NATARAJAN: Dear, your anger was thoroughly justified. I'm cool. I need to understand my daughter's feelings. You take any call what your mind says. Okay.

RADHA: Thank you so much, pa. You and amma have sacrificed so much for my upbringing.

NATARAJAN: Sweetie, my heart is filled with everlasting joy seeing your status today. My blessings will always be with you, even after I depart. I will see you from above. I'll always be with you, dear. Don't worry.

Radha becomes emotional now to the heart-touching statements of her father.

RADHA: Appa, please pa. I love you. You are making me cry with your words.

NATARAJAN: No, sweetie. You shouldn't cry. You should know how to handle things boldly in life, come what may. Okay!

RADHA (wiping her eyes): Okay, pa. I'll not cry. Yes, you have trained me to be a bold lady. Did you have breakfast, pa?

NATARAJAN: I will have it now. Seetha is preparing. Don't worry, dear. I'm okay. Be calm. Concentrate on your work. Okay!

RADHA: Okay, pa. Take care.

She hangs her phone. Closing her eyes with both hands, she cries. Reality is hitting her hard. After a few seconds, she gets up and goes to Sunitha's workstation. Sunitha gets up, seeing her boss approaching.

SUNITHA: Ma'am, are you okay? Are you in tears? You look different today.

RADHA: I'm okay, Sunitha. I just became emotional interacting with my father. I'll go to the guest room for some time. If Kishore comes, tell him.

SUNITHA: Sure, ma'am. (*After a slight pause*) Ma'am, you have been an inspiration to all of us. You showed us how to be courageous and bold. Now, I have tears seeing you in tears.

RADHA: I'm a daughter to a loving father. I'll only see him for a few more days in his life.

SUNITHA (stunned): Ma'am!

RADHA (tearfully): Father has 4th-stage metastatic cancer. It is spreading fast. His survival is another 6 to 12 months maximum. Sunitha, before I break down, I'll leave. I don't have the mind to work today. Anything important, call me. Tell Kishore, please.

SUNITHA: Okay, ma'am. Take care.

Radha slowly leaves towards the main door. Sunitha is wiping her eyes. Radha is a positive beacon ray of light for her colleagues. Her mere presence is enough to motivate them to excel. Radha knows how to bring the best out of her team. She will go out of her way to help them. As such, her colleagues have an emotional bonding with her. A picture-perfect team leader.

SCENE 18: INTERIOR, HIGH TECH GLOBAL HEALTHCARE SOLUTIONS, GUEST ROOM – MORNING

Radha is gently reclining on the posh sofa with her legs on the table and two arms behind her head. It looks like she is in deep slumber or thinking with closed eyes. Then, suddenly, there is a knocking sound on the door. Radha gets a bit jolted by the sound.

RADHA: Yes, please come in.

Kishore gently walks in. Radha gets up seeing her boss.

KISHORE: Hey! What happened? Are you okay?

Without speaking a word, Radha slowly falls onto his chest and cries. Kishore is stunned. He has not seen Radha like this.

KISHORE: Radha, come on. Why are you crying! I'm here to help you. Don't worry.

Kishore makes her sit on the couch, and he goes to the phone. He picks the receiver and dials.

KISHORE: Kishore here. Get two coffee and biscuits to Guest room 303. Thank you.

Radha narrates the events that unfolded last evening to Kishore with a sad look. He gives a patient listening. Radha is in tears. He can understand her feelings and also the feelings of her parents. He gently keeps his hand on Radha's right palm and looks at her.

KISHORE: Radha, I can understand your predicament.

There is a knocking sound on the door.

KISHORE: Please, come in.

With a gentle smile, the waiter comes inside with a tray containing two cups of coffee and biscuits and leaves the room gracefully. Kishore hands over a cup to Radha. Sipping the coffee slowly, Kishore looks at Radha.

KISHORE: Radha, I like you a lot. I only wish I had you as my wife.

Radha looks at him silently.

KISHORE: My parents are coming as a stumbling block. They like you so much, but your Sevvai dhosham is not going well with them. They are highly religious and spiritual. Moreover, my father will discuss it with his family members. They will brainwash him not to proceed. Whether we like it or not, horoscope matching is still prevalent in our community.

RADHA: Please, Kishore. I'm sick of this Sevvai dhosham issue.

KISHORE: Radha, let me discuss with them for one last time. Let me see if I can convince them. Give me a day. If I am unsuccessful, I suggest you go ahead with Mahesh's proposal. I'll not feel bad.

Radha places her hand on Kishore's hand and looks at him enticingly.

KISHORE: Radha, you know about gossip mongers. You coming into my life will make many elders in my family gossip and inject poison into my father's mind. When elders don't have any job, their best time is to gossip.

RADHA: Please don't push your parents against the wall. No. Don't do that. It will disturb them if you revolt against their beliefs and thoughts. I would feel blessed to have you as my life partner. Kishore, you are a part of my family in many ways. My parents would feel fortunate to have you as their son-in-law. You are their pet.

Kishore gets up and extends his right hand.

KISHORE: Get up. Be cheerful. Your charming face is your biggest strength and asset. If the forces above decide, then we will unite somehow. Don't worry. Get up.

Radha, with renewed confidence, gets up, and both leave the room cheerfully.

CHAPTER 6

SCENE 19: EXTERIOR, BLUE BAY VIEW RESTAURANT, ELLIOTS BEACH – EVENING

Mahesh, a six-footer gentleman smartly dressed in his formal executive attire, looks trendy in his dark brown pants and a matching light brown striped full-sleeve shirt. He is eagerly waiting for Radha's arrival. This evening will be the first rendezvous between Mahesh and Radha. Radha has, in a way, given due respect to her father's desire to look at this prospective groom. She has a soft fondness for Kishore, but that is out of her reach now, given his family predicament and superstitious beliefs. Kishore couldn't convince his parents and, in particular, his father. Kishore didn't want any bad name and image to come on Radha. As such, he convinced Radha to go ahead and look at Mahesh as her life partner.

Radha graciously halts her SUV in front of the restaurant. Stepping out of her SUV, she spots Mahesh approaching her with a soft smile. Gently, he comes near the door to receive her. Radha emerges smilingly with her posh small leather shoulder bag drooping down her body elegantly.

MAHESH: Hi! Radha. Nice to meet you.

RADHA (smilingly): Pleasure to meet you, Mahesh. Extremely sorry I was late by a few minutes.

MAHESH: No issues, Radha. Even I arrived before ten minutes only. So come, let's get in.

SCENE 20: INTERIOR, BLUE BAY VIEW RESTAURANT, ELLIOTS BEACH – EVENING

The manager of the restaurant, smartly dressed in a full suit, ushers them and shows them a pleasant corner table overlooking the beautiful Bay of Bengal. Indeed, a wonderful setting for the first meeting for the prospective minds to merge in the sea of tranquillity, future dreams, hopes, and aspirations. The dim glow of the lights above gives the necessary warmth feelings.

MANAGER: Sir, would you like to go for some starters.

MAHESH: Any veg speciality?

MANAGER: Would you like to taste mint-keera vada, cashew pakora or pepper masala corn kernels with tangy sauce?

RADHA: Oh! Good combination.

Radha, in a subtle way, gives her endorsement and liking. Mahesh, being an intelligent person, latches on to her preference.

MAHESH: We will have a plate of all three. Main dishes, we will order after some time.

Mahesh has discretely indicated to the manager that he wants privacy and needs quality time with his friend.

MANAGER: Fine, sir.

The manager takes leave smilingly.

RADHA (curiously): So, how was your day?

MAHESH: Oh! Hectic day. Sales closing. Usual pressure from head office to do more. Handling FMCG products is an intense pressure job.

RADHA: Well, we go through the same thing. Sales pressure is always there. By the way, I use a few of your company products.

MAHESH: Oh! So nice. You are our valuable customer then.

RADHA: Your skin and hair care products are so good. Pleasant and soothing. I have recommended it to a few colleagues too.

MAHESH: That's so nice of you. Appreciate it.

RADHA: Looks like your company is the market leader!

MAHESH: We have worked hard to reach that position. Our customer's endorsement of quality and word of mouth is the reason for our success. When we have customers like you, we are bound to taste success.

Mahesh and Radha are setting up an excellent platform and wavelength for them to springboard to the next level of discussion.

MAHESH: So, you handle healthcare industry software products.

RADHA: Well, we handle a gamut of software applications for the entire healthcare industry. We do projects for manufacturing, sales, distribution, and manage complete IT requirements for big global hospital chains. The uniqueness is that we offer one-stop-shop customer-friendly applications. That's our USP. Like your organisation, we have a leadership position in this significant domain.

MAHESH: Oh! That's great. So, you also tour officially.

Mahesh is trying to probe in slowly.

RADHA: Yes. To some extent. I handle Southeast Asian countries. Visit Singapore, Indonesia, Malaysia, and Thailand. The majority of the jobs we finish online.

MAHESH: Great!

RADHA: How about you.

MAHESH: I look after the entire South Indian region and Defence canteen business. Also, handle all India training. Ten days a month, I tour. My senior management wants me to relocate to head office in Mumbai. They have offered Chief General Manager, Marketing for personal hygiene products. I've declined the offer.

RADHA: Big post. Why did you decline?

MAHESH: Well, I prefer to stay in Chennai.

The waiter, accompanied by the manager, comes with a big tray. He keeps the dishes on the table.

MANAGER: Sir, I will get the main course in half an hour. Or you want it early.

MAHESH: Please serve us after thirty minutes. The starters are good enough until then.

MANAGER: Okay, sir.

Mahesh looks at Radha.

MAHESH: Please, have.

Radha slowly takes a spoon full of corn kernels to her mouth.

RADHA: Oh my God! It's yummy. Very tasty.

Listening to Radha, Mahesh reciprocates by having a spoon full.

MAHESH: Yes, really tangy.

RADHA: Mahesh, can I ask you something personal?

MAHESH: Sure.

RADHA: Do you smoke regularly?

This question surprises Mahesh.

MAHESH: Yes. Have a few in a day. Any issues?

RADHA: I'm deadly allergic to cigarette smoke. How many do you have?

MAHESH (hesitantly): Seven to ten a day.

RADHA: My God! Seven to ten a day! Is it not harmful? I'm okay with drinks but not cigarettes. I get a headache.

MAHESH: I'm used to it. I cannot leave it just like that. To be candid, it is like a good companion.

RADHA: Mahesh, I would like to place my cards clearly before we can consider the next step.

MAHESH: Sure. No issues. Go ahead.

Radha keeps seeing the plate with mint-keera vada.

RADHA: Look, Mahesh. My father is counting his final days due to 4th-stage cancer. He wants to see me get married. That's his prayers and wish. It so happened that both of us have Sevvai dhosham in our horoscope. Hence, we got matched, at least on paper.

MAHESH: Okay, what are you trying to drive home the point?

Radha looks at Mahesh in a subdued manner.

RADHA (hesitantly): Candidly speaking, I'm not interested in marriage.

MAHESH (bit stunned): Oh! Then why are we meeting?

RADHA: I am fed up and tired of many people rejecting me because of my Sevvai dhosham. However, I have agreed to meet you and see if something works. I want to satisfy my father's wishes and requests.

MAHESH: That Sevvai dhosham is a bloody curse on both of us. Prospective people reject us just because of this horoscope defect! Absolute crap. Well, I don't want to be too critical. It is astrological science. There could be some meaning to it that we don't know properly.

RADHA (surprised): So, you believe in astrology?

MAHESH: Radha, our traditional belief system stems only from pure science. That's the beauty. Please don't think negatively about having Sevvai dhosham. Look, God gave us many beautiful gifts. Right! Did God not give us a good education, decent job, fantastic lifestyle and an image apart from Sevvai dhosham? Because of Sevvai dhosham, God has made us come together today. Don't you think so? Okay, let's not get bogged by this defect.

Radha gives a patient listening to the wisdom of thoughts flowing from Mahesh.

MAHESH: What if we don't settle in our personal life? We can still lead a great life in many ways. Isn't it!

RADHA: Well, I endorse your views. It makes sense. I like your positive approach. Excellent quality, Mahesh.

MAHESH (apologetically): Thank you, Radha, for your sweet comments. Due apologies if my statements hurt you in any way. Okay, let's leave this topic. Move on.

RADHA: Look, Mahesh. I'm not a traditional brahmin girl. However, I'm spiritual but not religious. My spiritual outlook is simple. I am an ardent devotee of Lord Ganesh. I tell him the good, bad or ugly things in my life. Because of my higher education in the US and my corporate lifestyle visiting many countries, I am a blend of modernity and the Indian value system and ethos to some extent.

MAHESH: Okay, fine.

RADHA: If we settle by God's grace, I don't want any unnecessary pressure from your parents towards my lifestyle. I'm making this very clear.

Having a bite of mint keera vada, Mahesh is silently listening to her views.

RADHA: I wear western dresses. I don't want any comments on my dress sense. For that matter, even my parents have not objected until this day. They admire my dress. I hate anyone talking at my back.

MAHESH: Fine.

RADHA: I value my corporate career. I am a highly career-oriented person. I am doing pretty good with God's grace and blessings. Well, I have a very bright future in my professional life. My organisation has big plans for me. So, I don't want any disturbances in my marital life that would affect my professional career.

MAHESH: Okay, fine. I hope you will give due respect to your in-laws.

RADHA: What do you mean by giving due respect? I don't get you.

MAHESH: What a normal daughter-in-law is supposed to give in our traditional culture.

RADHA: Mahesh, your parents, need to earn respect, not demand or command. It will not work with me. They can't force things on me. They will find me as a beautiful daughter-in-law if they are good to me. Well, more than a daughter-in-law, I'll be even like a daughter to them. I'll treat them like my parents. I can vouch for that.

MAHESH: Okay. I get your point.

Radha is making many aspects crystal clear. She doesn't want to unnecessarily neck into a marital relationship to settle in her life and fulfil her father's dreams and wishes. Inwardly, she has a fear of committing to this relationship. Relishing the starters, she looks at Mahesh intermittently.

RADHA: Look, Mahesh. I am a socialite and party a lot with my colleagues and friends. I hope you are not possessive. Equally, I'll not interfere in your other aspects of personal life. You can socialise in any way you want. Be faithful to your wife; that's it. But don't smoke in front of me.

MAHESH: Fair enough. Appreciate your views.

RADHA: Since I am the only daughter, I will spend time equally with my parents. I want to be close to my father during his last days. Look, Mahesh, my parents mean so much in my life. What I am today is because of them.

MAHESH: Well, I can understand your situation. No issues.

RADHA: Mahesh, you want to say something, tell now itself. You can be point blank with me. No issues. By the way, are you a moody person?

MAHESH (shocked): Oh! Me moody! Not at all. I was giving a patient listening to you. (*After a slight pause*) Radha, I appreciate your openness and frank talk. Good that you made things clear. I don't have any issues. Both of us are good professionals. Well, we need to understand each other to lead life harmoniously. We have to make slight adjustments here and there since we embark on a new life journey. Do you agree?

RADHA: Absolutely. No issues.

As agreed, after thirty minutes, the waiter brings the tray containing the food ordered and serves them enthusiastically. Mahesh and Radha seem to relish the food. It looks like their first meeting has gone pretty well with open communication. Radha has a feeling that Mahesh has endorsed her views in principle. After dinner, both agree to catch up for the next meeting date to understand each other better.

SCENE 21: EXTERIOR, BLUE BAY VIEW RESTAURANT, ELLIOTS BEACH – EVENING

Radha and Mahesh leave the restaurant relaxed, having gone through the first round of a fruitful discussion. Mahesh sees Radha.

MAHESH: Radha, just a minute. I'll go to my car.

RADHA (smilingly): Please.

Radha looks at the buzzing activity with many youngsters partying at different restaurants along the promenade. Mahesh comes with a bag.

MAHESH: Radha, just a small gift for you.

RADHA (flabbergasted): Oh! Calvin Klein Eternity! Why all these formalities, Mahesh?

MAHESH: I just felt like giving it on the first date.

RADHA: Oh! So nice of you, dear. Thank you so much. Appreciate it.

MAHESH: This is a gift from our company for being a loyal customer.

Mahesh Gives Radha a gift pack containing skin and hair care products. Radha is stunned by the hospitality.

RADHA: Thank you so much. Shit. I don't have anything to give you. I just came straight from my office. Well, I can offer you a sweet kiss.

Radha gently hugs Mahesh and gives him a sweet kiss. The wonderful kiss has undoubtedly sent 100 watts of power into Mahesh's body to rejuvenate. People passing by see the bonhomie and affection between them. It has caught many eyes. Mahesh accompanies Radha to her SUV. She bids farewell and graciously drives away.

CHAPTER 7

SCENE 22: INTERIOR, JOE & SHAN LTD, OFFICE – MORNING

Mahesh walks elegantly into the sprawling office, wearing trendy black pants and a black striped white shirt. Many colleagues greet him. His Secretary, Stella, a modern female with a good dress sense, is seriously looking into the computer screen and typing. She adorns a nice black T-shirt matching her below-knee steel-grey skirt and a small scarf around her neck to lift her demeanour. Mahesh slowly comes towards his cabin.

MAHESH: Stella! Good morning.

Stella softly looks up. Her eyes look watery after seeing her boss!

STELLA: Hi! Good morning.

MAHESH: Stella, can you come into my cabin after a while. I need to talk to you.

STELLA: Sure. After 10 minutes. I'll finish sending the mail to Head Office. Furnishing them the latest figures.

MAHESH: Fine. No issues. Tell cafeteria people to send two coffees.

STELLA: Sure.

Mahesh gently opens the door of his cabin and gets inside. Stella is looking at her fingers, looking lost in something. She keeps rubbing it. After a few minutes, Mahesh comes out.

MAHESH: Stella, I'll go to the terrace.

STELLA (soberly): Okay.

MAHESH: I will be back in 15 to 20 minutes.

Stella looks at him and nods her head in affirmative. Then, without winking her eyes, she looks at Mahesh leaving the hall.

SCENE 23: EXTERIOR, JOE & SHAN LTD, OFFICE TERRACE – MORNING

Mahesh stylishly lights his Marlboro cigarette, a typical symbol of masculine pride. He looks down the busy traffic flowing on the famous Chennai Mount Road from his seven-storied exclusive integrated office building. Smoking is not allowed inside the office area, and if at all someone wants to fag, they come to the terrace. The terrace looks quite cosy, with a few small canopies erected for people to sit under and refresh. Srikanth, Regional Manager, skincare products, comes with a smile. Srikanth reports to Mahesh. Mahesh shows him the Marlboro cigarette packet. Srikanth elegantly picks a cigarette, and Mahesh ignites it with his lighter. Both of them occupy the chairs around a circular table. Blissfully puffing the Marlboro,

MAHESH: Sri, how is it going?

SRIKANTH: Mahi, Kerala and TN achieved. Hopefully, Karnataka and Andhra will be through by tomorrow evening. We are expecting orders today. Stella has processed yesterday's orders.

MAHESH: That's good, Sri.

SRIKANTH: Mahi, my guys are slogging their ass out.

MAHESH: Sri, your team is doing good. Mark my word; they will get recognition. Good performers will be encouraged.

SRIKANTH: Thanks, Mahi.

MAHESH: Okay, I'll get going. Buddy, we need to catch up for a drink one of these days. After monthly closing, organise one for our team.

SRIKANTH: Sure, mate.

SCENE 24: INTERIOR, JOE & SHAN LTD, MAHESH'S CABIN – MORNING

Mahesh is seriously looking into the computer. He dials his intercom phone.

MAHESH: Stella, can you come in.

After a few seconds, Stella gently enters the cabin and takes her seat. Her charming face looks dull, conveying some subtle emotional feelings. She keeps looking down.

MAHESH: Stella!

Now Stella looks up.

MAHESH: Stella, are you cut with me?

STELLA (delicately): How was your first date with Radha?

MAHESH: Pretty good. Brilliant female.

STELLA: Mahi, Radha is a perfect match for you. She has beauty with a brain. High flier. Not like me. Just remove me from your mind.

MAHESH: Are you feeling cheated? Humm!

Stella doesn't respond. She is about to break down, but she is controlling her emotions.

STELLA: It is my bloody mistake …. I madly fell in love with you. I enjoyed you.

MAHESH: Stella, I loved you to the core. You know. My parents are coming our way. Well, my mother is an orthodox brahmin. She will not accept a Christian daughter-in-law in the family. So, if I have to settle with you, I must leave them. We can't stay in the same house.

Stella starts crying. She is not able to hold anymore. Mahesh gently gets up from his seat. He gently hugs her. She hugs his waist.

MAHESH: Stella, I love you, dear.

Mahesh keeps hugging and patting her shoulder.

MAHESH: Stella, the mistake is with me. I enticed you.

Mahesh lifts her head.

MAHESH: Stella, tell me. Shall I call off the proposal? I don't want to ditch you. You mean so much to my life, dear.

Stella, with tears, hugs Mahesh.

STELLA: No, Mahesh. You settle with Radha. Give happiness to your parents, Radha, and her family.

MAHESH: What will you do?

Stella is silent for some time. She looks up.

STELLA: The Lord will show me some way. I have faith in him. He will not leave me alone.

Hearing this, Mahesh hugs her.

MAHESH: Stella, I feel guilty.

STELLA: No, Mahesh. You were true to me all these days. I have enjoyed your company.

MAHESH: I moved with you so close because I couldn't find a suitable partner in my life. Courtesy of my horoscope defect. You came in nicely into my life, dear. But I feel I am letting you down.

STELLA: Now, you have found a beautiful female to come into your life. Utilise the God-given opportunity. Just enjoy, Mahesh.

MAHESH: If I settle with Radha, how will you take it up?

STELLA: Nothing is working in my mind. I feel like quitting the job and doing some service in the Church. Serving the Lord will give me happiness in some way.

Hugging Stella,

MAHESH: No, Stella. You will not leave me. I need you badly. Please, it is my request. Your presence here will rejuvenate me. I beg you. Stay with me. It will disturb me a lot if your company is not here. No Stella, don't leave.

Stella hugs Mahesh with tears rolling.

STELLA: Mahesh, my presence will corrupt your mind. You have to be true to Radha. Mahi, you can't have two ladies in your life.

MAHESH: Okay, we will go out in the evening. Let's get to our job. We have to close our sales tomorrow. Come on. Get up.

Stella gets up. Mahesh gives her a gentle, sweet kiss.

SCENE 25: INTERIOR, RIVER VIEW APARTMENTS, RADHA'S FLAT, LIVING HALL – EVENING

After a month

Kishore is sitting in the main hall with Radha's parents. Seated next to Natarajan, he seems to be discussing harmoniously.

KISHORE (*looking at Natarajan*): Uncle, you don't worry about marriage. I'll conduct it along with my team. Radha is like a sister to me. I want aunty and you to relax.

Natarajan keeps his hand on Kishore's thigh.

NATARAJAN: Kishore, I don't know how to thank you. I don't have words.

SEETHA: Kishore, you are like a son to us. We are blessed to have your association.

KISHORE: Aunty, I have finalised AVM Rajeswari marriage hall and a well-known caterer. Radha is a darling to us in our office. We will ensure her marriage is grand in all aspects. Many senior executives from Mumbai are eager to attend her wedding.

Natarajan, in tears, holds Kishore's hands.

NATARAJAN: Kishore, please take care of Radha when I pass away. I want you to be close to her all the time.

Kishore holds Natarajan's hands in reciprocation.

KISHORE: Uncle, don't worry about anything. Don't think of your health. You'll live longer.

Radha comes with a tray from the kitchen with bowls containing Gulab Jamun sweet. She serves them.

CHAPTER 8

SCENE 26: INTERIOR, CITADEL SQUARE APARTMENT, MAHESH'S FLAT – EVENING

Three months have gone by after the grand wedding between Radha and Mahesh. Both of them are sitting perpendicular and having food in the dining hall. Radha's in-laws, Moorthy and Lalitha (nickname – Lalli), are in the living room, enthusiastically watching a Tamil TV episode. For elders, it is a great relaxation to view the never-ending serials shown on the TV. For them, it is like an elixir of life. The beauty is that they carry the message from the TV shows seriously as if it severely impacts their lives. Radha is wearing a causal full skirt and a matching loose pink cotton shirt. Mahesh is in his trendy half Adidas trousers and a black striped T-shirt. Radha eagerly takes a scoop of sambar (side dish) and pours it into his plate.

RADHA: Want some more?

MAHESH: No, Thanks.

Radha pours into her plate also and relishes the taste of soft idlis. Suddenly the mobile phone kept on top of the fridge rings. Radha picks it up and sees the caller's name. She sees Mahesh.

RADHA: Ashok on the line.

Radha hands over the mobile to Mahesh.

MAHESH: Hi Ashok!

Mahesh is giving a patient listening for a few seconds. Radha is looking at him inconspicuously.

MAHESH: Ashok, please don't give shit excuses. You need to finish your target at any cost.

Radha looks at his different tone and tenor. Mahesh's father, Moorthy, lowers the TV volume to ensure his son doesn't get agitated.

MAHESH: Ashok, you have been repeating this excuse often for not doing your target. I cannot accept this anymore. I have been patient with you all these days.

With his mobile tucked to his ears with his fingers, Mahesh gets up from his chair and keeps walking inside the dining hall restlessly. His parents are keenly watching in silence.

MAHESH: Ashok, just put in your papers if you cannot finish the target this time. I can't show any more leniency to you. Other team members are slogging their balls out, and you have taken it easy in your life. Quit the job if you are not interested in working. I'll relieve you immediately and settle your accounts. Okay!

Mahesh disconnects the call, goes to the washbasin and rinses his mouth.

RADHA: Mahesh, finish it.

MAHESH: No, thanks. I'm through.

Mahesh takes the plate with two leftover idlis. He is about to discard it in the dust bin.

RADHA: Mahesh, wait. I'll have it. We can't throw food like that.

Mahesh heeding her words keeps the plate on the table. He leaves the dining hall with his mood disturbed. Mahesh's parents are watching the happenings and are not looking comfortable. Radha is eating silently.

SCENE 27: INTERIOR, CITADEL SQUARE APARTMENT, MAHESH'S BEDROOM – NIGHT

Radha is reclining on the bed with a pillow to support her. With her laptop on her thigh, she is seriously watching the screen. Through the big glass door dividing the balcony and the bedroom, Radha sees Mahesh having a fag. Radha has made it explicitly clear that Mahesh should not smoke inside the room when she is there. Mahesh chucks the cigarette into the ashtray. After a few minutes, he slowly opens the door to come in. Radha immediately coughs a few times. The cigarette smell has diffused into the room fast due to the heavy wind blowing. Mahesh picks up a magazine on the table. He comes and reclines next to Radha and curiously sees the magazine. Radha casually looks at Mahesh.

RADHA: Hi!

MAHESH: Humm.

Mahesh doesn't look at her straight.

RADHA: Why is it you are so moody?

MAHESH: Only you feel like that.

RADHA: I'm telling you because I feel like that.

MAHESH: Bloody Ashok screwed my dinner.

RADHA: Well, I don't want to comment on that. It is not my business. Okay, let me concentrate on my slides.

Radha keeps seeing the laptop seriously and

RADHA: Slide 23, good…24, good…25, good. Fantastic!

Radha closes her laptop blissfully and keeps it inside the cute-looking bag. She gets up gently and places the laptop bag on the table. Radha picks a moisturiser bottle from the dressing table and sits on the bed relaxedly. She frees her tresses to comfort. After applying the moisturiser gently to her face, arms, and legs, she slowly lies on the bed seeing the ceiling. The beautiful fragrance of the moisturiser has dispersed quite nicely into the room. Mahesh looks at her.

MAHESH: You want me to switch off the lights!

RADHA: If you don't mind, please. I need to sleep and get up early. Have an important presentation tomorrow.

MAHESH: Okay.

Heeding her request, Mahesh keeps the book on the table and switches off the room lights. The night lamp is burning softly near the bathroom. Mahesh comes and lounges close to Radha. After a few minutes, he slowly puts his right arm over her shoulder and hugs her gently.

RADHA: Mahesh, please.

Mahesh is in no mood to let his hand go from her. Radha is also feeling a little comfortable with his hug. Now, Mahesh slowly advances his face and kisses Radha's cheek softly. Radha gets aroused and swirls her body. Mahesh is trying to smooch her. She turns her head away. Mahesh makes repeated attempts, but she is not yielding.

RADHA: No smooch, Mahesh…. Please, don't do it. I dislike the cigarette smell in your mouth. I'm allergic, please.

Radha pushes him sideways. She takes a big blanket and pulls it over her body. Mahesh doesn't want to move any further in his romantic adventures with Radha, knowing it would backfire. So, he also pulls his blanket and sleeps sideways, facing the wall.

SCENE 28: INTERIOR, CITADEL SQUARE APARTMENT, BALCONY – MORNING

Radha and Mahesh, looking relaxed sitting on the lovely spacious balcony, seem to enjoy the fresh morning breeze flowing from the riverside. Sipping the morning pure filter coffee, Mahesh is grazing through the headlines of THE TIMES OF INDIA newspaper. Radha is enjoying the scenic beauty. Mahesh's mobile rings. He picks it up.

MAHESH: Mr. Guptha, good morning.

Mahesh is giving a patient listening. Radha picks up THE HINDU newspaper and is keenly interested in reading a front-page article.

MAHESH: Mr. Guptha, I'll try to do another three crores because of your request. Five will be very tough to squeeze my team. This month my target is a bit high. I hope my team will achieve 75 crores. I am confident that we will pull through. So, I will commit three for you. Gupthaji, next month my target is 75 again. It will put enormous pressure.

Again, he gives a patient listening.

MAHESH: I'll call you by 5 pm. You can take my words for granted. Let me see if I can do anything extra. Cheers, boss.

Mahesh keeps the mobile on the round-shaped coffee table. Radha sees him curiously.

MAHESH: My Vice President, Guptha. He is requesting I do five crores extra this month. Mumbai region is down by ten crores.

RADHA: Oh my God! It is 7:15 am. I need to rush up. Okay, I'll get going.

SCENE 29: INTERIOR, CITADEL SQUARE APARTMENT, DINING HALL – MORNING

Radha, dressed smartly in bluish-black pants and a light green shirt, is in a hurry. She opens the fridge and takes two small vegetable and fruit salad boxes. She places it into her bag. Then, she enters the pooja room to offer her silent prayers for a few seconds and applies the sacred ash and kumkum. Mahesh's mother, Lalitha, comes from the other bedroom. She is surprised to see Radha packing her bags and about to leave.

LALITHA: Radha, breakfast is ready.

RADHA: Thanks, ma. I am in a hurry. I have an important meeting.

LALITHA: If you wait for five minutes, I'll get it.

RADHA: No, ma. I need to leave immediately; otherwise, I'll get caught in the mad traffic.

LALITHA: I prepared the dough last night, thinking you would have hot pooris and sabzi now.

RADHA: Amma, please don't prepare anything for me. I'll take care of myself. I've requested you many times not to do.

Radha quickly takes her bag and leaves the main hall. Lalitha is looking dejected. She looks at her husband, Moorthy, who is seriously reading the newspaper in the living room. Unnoticed, he has been silently watching the proceedings. Lalitha goes near her husband.

LALITHA: Don't know why she is like this? I prepared dough yesterday, thinking she would have pooris for breakfast.

MOORTHY: Lalli, mind your business. No one asked you to prepare.

LALITHA (stunned): Oh!

MOORTHY: She's not a baby.

Lalitha stares at her husband. She is visibly upset with the way he is talking.

LALITHA: I need to hit my mind with a slipper.

MOORTHY: Don't say. Please do it.

Lalitha is speechless. She expected consoling words from her husband, but it has turned the other way around. So now, she proceeds towards the balcony where Mahesh is having a fag.

LALITHA: Radha has left without having breakfast.

MAHESH: She has an important meeting today. She got late.

LALITHA: If she had told me earlier, I would have prepared and kept it ready.

MAHESH: Okay, maa. Don't brood. Just leave it.

Lalitha is silently looking at her son.

MAHESH: Amma, if you don't mind, can you get me a cup of coffee.

LALITHA: Radha didn't give you?

MAHESH: I had. I need one more.

LALITHA (impulsively): I don't understand what life you people lead! You go in one direction. Then, she goes the other way.

MAHESH (furiously): Amma! Please! Learn to put a full stop to a sentence. I'm going through this piece of shit every day!

Lalitha is silent and keeps seeing her son dejectedly.

MAHESH (angrily): Earlier, you didn't want a Christian daughter-in-law in the family. Because of you people, I didn't marry Stella. Now, you have a daughter-in-law from the same community. You cannot get along with her also.

Lalitha doesn't utter a word. Instead, she is digesting the words spewing out from her son. Mahesh looks at his mother heatedly.

MAHESH: I think I made a big mistake. I should have taken a separate house and stayed. This mother-in-law, daughter-in-law conflict will never end in this world. Amma, try to change if you want peace and respect in this family. Please understand that your daughter-in-law is highly qualified and well-travelled. She has seen enough world than what we have seen. So, don't give sermons to her.

Lalitha feels she has had enough from him. She slowly and tearfully walks away without responding to her son's outburst.

CHAPTER 9

SCENE 30: INTERIOR, HIGH TECH GLOBAL HEALTHCARE SOLUTIONS, CONFERENCE HALL – MORNING

Senior executives smartly dressed in full suits eagerly look towards the presentation board. Next to Kishore, the chair is empty. Then, we hear the voice of Radha in the background. As we pan from left to right, Radha comes into the frame, looking elegant, confident, and optimistic in her outlook.

RADHA: This application will help track the consignment on a real-time basis. We are interfacing both international and domestic routes. As a result, the regional offices will know the probable date of stock arrival and plan their order scheduling accordingly.

Sunil Tandon, the President, is watching Radha's presentation sitting adjacent to Raghav, Regional Director, Chennai region.

SUNIL TANDON: Radha, how about the major hospital chain? Are we interfacing the hospital with our key distributors and our office?

RADHA (smilingly): Yes, Mr. Tandon. Many functionalities are getting interfaced so that we get the exact picture. We are also incorporating statistical applications to generate MIS reports.

SUNIL TANDON: Oh! That's fantastic. I appreciate you thinking out of the box about many things. That's the way to go forward and help our customers.

RADHA: Well, that concludes my presentation. I am confident that my team will roll out the application and make it operational next month.

SUNIL TANDON: Brilliant, Radha. I like your dynamism. Keep that positive spirit alive and kicking. Okay! You are a valuable asset to our organisation. We have big plans for you, Radha. Any help you want, just put it forward. We will do our best to keep you and your team happy. We want you to feel comfortable. Okay. Cheers.

SCENE 31: INTERIOR, HIGH TECH GLOBAL HEALTHCARE SOLUTIONS, DINING HALL – AFTERNOON

Radha is exuberantly having a buffet lunch in the company of Raghav and Kishore. Sunil Tandon slowly sneaks in with his plate smilingly and sees Radha.

SUNIL TANDON: Hi! Charming! You made an excellent presentation today. Your charm reverberates in this Chennai office in many ways.

RADHA (smilingly): Oh! Thank you, Mr. Tandon.

SUNIL TANDON: Radha, very soon you will hear the big news. Watch out!

RADHA: Too much suspense!

SUNIL TANDON: Wait, dear. It is worth the wait.

RADHA: Okay. Cool.

SCENE 32: INTERIOR, CITADEL SQUARE APARTMENT, MAHESH'S FLAT – DINING HALL – AFTERNOON

As we cut across to Mahesh's apartment, Moorthy and Lalitha are having their lunch unassumingly. Lalitha is pouring rasam (spicy lentil water) into Moorthy's plate.

MOORTHY: Enough! Enough.

As Moorthy is slowly relishing the rasam rice,

LALITHA: My mind is disturbed.

MOORTHY: Dear, don't brood in front of food? Quietly eat.

Lalitha takes a scoop of rasam and pours it into her plate.

LALITHA: I don't like certain things in this house.

MOORTHY (little annoyed): Are you okay! Humm! Have you gone mad or what?

LALITHA: Peace has gone out of this house after Mahesh got married.

MOORTHY: You mind your business peace will be there.

LALITHA: So, you're blaming me. Are you not seeing what is going on in this house?

MOORTHY: Look, chant Rama Krishna and lead your life. Don't poke your nose into their issues.

LALITHA: Even my friends in this building are indirectly commenting on the dresses worn by Radha. She can be a bit decent in her dress.

MOORTHY (angrily): You ladies don't have any business in your lives. Being idle, you people enter into all sorts of gossip. Radha will wear or not wear any dress; what bothers them?

After listening to Lalitha's ranting, Moorthy takes the rasam rice to his mouth wrathfully. But unfortunately, a few rice particles stick to his lips and outer mouth.

MOORTHY: Look, your friends are jealous that your daughter-in-law is beautiful, gorgeous, highly qualified, has a big job, is modern and driving a posh SUV. They don't have one like what you have. They will comment on whatever they want. Then, like an idiot, you believe their words and grumble with me. Just show me one female like Radha in this apartment. Feel proud you have a wonderful daughter-in-law.

Lalitha is silent. She has received enough messages from her hubby.

MOORTHY: Have you ever seen me uttering a word? Humm! Instead of talking, take tuition to a few poor school students. You will find happiness doing charitable work. Use your good education for good things in life. Not for brooding. Okay!

Lalitha has received a good dose of vital sermons from her husband. Nevertheless, she remains silent and keeps eating.

SCENE 33: INTERIOR, JOE & SHAN LTD – AFTERNOON

Mahesh is in his cabin with two senior colleagues, Rajesh and Manoj. He has a few papers strewn on the table. Charming-looking Stella gently enters the room in her black midi skirt and striking yellow shirt. She places a few documents in front of Mahesh.

STELLA: Mahi, we have achieved 75.5. I have processed all orders received till last evening.

MAHESH: Fantastic, Stella!

MANOJ: Yesterday, Stella stayed until 10 pm. I dropped her.

MAHESH: Thank you, Stella. You deserve a big treat.

STELLA: Thank you, Mahi. If you give orders today, I'll process them. I've informed our warehouse people.

MAHESH: Rao from Hyderabad will call anytime. He is likely to give two crores extra. From Cochin and Bangalore, we are expecting one crore each. So final figure, I think we will touch 79 or 80 Crores. Guptha is so happy with our achievement.

STELLA: Evening dinner, shall I order Shanthi caterers? By the time we finish, it will be 9 or 10 pm.

MAHESH: Sure, Stella. Check numbers. Order dinner for our warehouse staff and other office staff.

Stella leaves the cabin gracefully.

RAJESH: Mahi, Stella is a tremendous asset to us. Yesterday, she was coordinating with the entire region for orders. She is the charming bridge in our team.

MAHESH: We need to recognise and reward her. It will happen soon. She is a significant pillar of strength to us. Guptha has approved my proposal for her elevation. Stella is likely to get the post of Regional Sales Coordinator.

MANOJ: Stella is worth it. She deserves it.

With Stella getting the elevation, she will bond more to the organisation. She passionately loves the work. But, no doubt, she has a beautiful boss through Mahesh. He has occupied a special place in her heart, which is precious to her.

SCENE 34: INTERIOR, HONDA CITY CAR – LATE EVENING

Mahesh slowly drives his Honda City car into a broad road and stops near Blue Diamond's apartment. Stella looks at him seducingly. Mahesh, during the drive, has hinted to her about the likely elevation to an executive position. Stella is on cloud nine.

STELLA: Mahi, if you don't mind, why don't you drop into my house for a few minutes. Please.

MAHESH: Seriously asking!

Stella keeps her right hand on Mahesh's thigh.

STELLA: Please, Mahi. You mean so much in my life. I want to spend a few minutes with you. Please, it is my humble request.

Mahesh gently drives the car into the guests' parking bays facing the apartment. He slowly comes out, and Stella ushers him into the gated community.

SCENE 35: INTERIOR, CITADEL SQUARE APARTMENT, MAHESH'S FLAT, LIVING HALL – LATE EVENING

It is 10:30 pm. Moorthy and Lalitha are watching the late evening Tamil TV serial. Radha enters the house silently by opening the door with her duplicate key. She sees her in-law's watching TV and doesn't utter a word. Straightaway, she heads to her bedroom. Lalitha looks at her husband.

LALITHA: Radha has gone to her room without speaking a word.

MOORTHY: You silently watch TV.

LALITHA: I have kept food on the table. I don't know if she is going to have dinner.

MOORTHY: Don't worry. If Radha and Mahesh don't consume it, we will give it to our watchman.

LALITHA (angrily): I don't prepare food for our watchman to eat.

MOORTHY: Okay, then keep it in the fridge. I'll consume it tomorrow.

LALITHA: I know you'll have it. Even if I keep poison, you'll drink it.

MOORTHY (sarcastically): That may be better than your food.

Moorthy sees her for a few seconds without winking his eyes.

MOORTHY: Can you just shut your mouth!

Lalitha keeps watching the TV with anger looming large on her face.

MOORTHY: Let the food be on the table. Don't go and check with Radha. I have a feeling she would have finished dinner outside.

LALITHA (angrily): I'm not preparing food from tomorrow onwards.

MOORTHY: Please do that.

LALITHA: Even you have your food outside.

MOORTHY: Good. I have been waiting all these days for you to say it. Good that you said it today. Appreciate it.

LALITHA: Only when you go out and have food, you'll know my value.

MOORTHY (sarcastically): I have been eating your food for the last 35 years. My taste buds have gone dry and numb. Even I need a change.

LALITHA: Instead of putting food for you, I can give it to our street dog, Jackie. He is trustworthy.

MOORTHY: Please give Jackie. I will go to the street and let Jackie occupy my place here if you want. Happy!

LALITHA: Happy.

Moorthy switches off the TV. He looks at his wife.

MOORTHY: Go to bed.

LALITHA: You go. I'll sleep here itself.

MOORTHY (sarcastically): Okay, fine. Have sweet dreams. Good night.

CHAPTER 10

SCENE 36: INTERIOR, CITADEL SQUARE APARTMENT, MAHESH'S FLAT, BEDROOM – LATE EVENING

Friday, February 15, 2019

Six months have passed by in the marital relationship between Radha and Mahesh. Unfortunately, things are not looking rosy in their life. There is a certain amount of discord brewing between them. However, life is pulling through despite hiccups. That's the beauty.

*10:30 pm. Radha comes out of the bathroom towelling her hair. She is seducingly beautiful in her nightgown and flowing hair. '**If I could tell you**', a soft, enticing Yanni's musical number is playing on the TV screen. For Radha, Yanni's music is like an amruth. Sitting on the dressing table couch, Radha does little makeup to look refreshing. Minutes later, from the small showcase, Radha picks up the novel '**The Mind and The Heart**' and goes to bed. Reclining softly with a pillow behind her, she is engrossed in reading the book with the side table lights on.*

After half an hour of serious reading, Radha gently lies sideways and pulls up her blanket. The night lamp is on, and Radha is in sound sleep. The novel is by the side of the table lamp. Presumably, Radha is having a sweet dream of what her mind and heart should do next!

At 12:15 am, Mahesh slowly sneaks into the bedroom. He gently opens the wardrobe and takes his dress. Then, quietly, he goes into the bathroom. After 20 minutes, Mahesh comes out of the bathroom dressed in brown striped half trousers and a matching T-shirt. He proceeds to the balcony to have a fag. Even the tiny sound of the bathroom door opening alerts Radha. In her subconscious mind, she can visualise Mahesh's presence. She pulls the blanket over her face again.

After a few minutes, Mahesh slowly comes and lies near Radha. He slowly puts his right hand around Radha's chest, and in the process, the blanket gets dislodged from her face. Suddenly Radha regains her senses and sneezes a few times. Her sensitive nose has caught the cigarette odour emanating from Mahesh. Then, Radha sees Mahesh by her side and his right hand on her chest. She annoyingly pushes away his hand and looks at him.

RADHA (angrily): Mahesh, what did you have?

MAHESH: Just a fag.

RADHA: No. Some other smell is coming. Did you have liquor?

MAHESH (hesitantly): Had a party.

RADHA: Then why did you lie? Oh! Shit! The smell is so strong. Did you have whiskey?

MAHESH: Yes.

Without uttering a word, Radha gets up. She takes a pillow and blanket and looks at Mahesh.

RADHA: My body has respect. Please don't come near me. I cannot take up the cigarette and liquor smell.

Radha walks away in a huff. She goes to the adjacent study room, which has a single cot. She lies on the cot and pulls the blanket over her face.

SCENE 37: INTERIOR, CITADEL SQUARE APARTMENT, MAHESH'S FLAT, LIVING ROOM – EARLY MORNING.

The rays of the dawn are slowly streaking through the balcony into the living room. The soothing music of M.S. Subbulakshmi's Vishnu Sahasranamam mantra reverberates and lifts the mood. Moorthy is reading the newspaper. Lalitha comes in a hurry and sees her husband.

LALITHA: Please get up.

MOORTHY: What happened?

LALITHA: Get up and come.

Moorthy, in silence, gets up and Lalitha ushers him to the small study room with the door partially opened. Radha is fast asleep. Both of them are stunned and return to the main hall.

MOORTHY: Lalli, don't bother. Maintain silence. Okay.

LALITHA: Things are not looking good at all.

MOORTHY: We don't know what happened!

LALITHA: I'm worried.

MOORTHY: Take it easy. Don't get perturbed.

LALITHA: It is hardly six months since they are married. I don't know how they are going to lead their life!

MOORTHY: Today's time is different to what we were living. Don't compare. Let us not poke our nose in their issue. They are mature enough to sort it out.

LALITHA: Then what are we here for as elders?

MOORTHY (furiously): Stupid! Radha has seen more world than what we have seen. Don't go and advise her on how to lead a life. You'll spoil your respect. Then don't brood after that.

LALITHA: I like the way you talk. Totally irresponsible! Mind you, you are her father-in-law!

MOORTHY: So, what? I don't want to spoil my relationship with her.

LALITHA: I know. You'll always support her. She is your pet.

MOORTHY: Have you gone mad! Humm! You'll not change in your life. Even God cannot change you. Try to earn respect from your daughter-in-law. Don't command and force things. It will not work.

Lalitha gives him a sarcastic look. She is definitely not happy with the response of her husband.

MOORTHY: Get me a good cup of coffee. Do that. I have been waiting for half an hour. Serve your husband first. Then think of others. Do you get me?

Lalitha silently goes to the kitchen.

SCENE 38: INTERIOR, CITADEL SQUARE APARTMENT, MAHESH'S FLAT, BEDROOM – MORNING.

Mahesh is sitting on the balcony and having a fag. Slowly, Radha comes into the bedroom with a pillow and a blanket. She sees Mahesh smoking happily. Angrily, she throws the pillow and blanket on the bed. Radha closes her bedroom door. Then, she goes to the balcony.

RADHA: Mahesh, can you come into the room. Want to talk to you.

MAHESH: What's it?

Mahesh chucks the cigarette into the ashtray and gently enters the room. Radha is sitting on the bed agitatedly, with Mahesh taking the chair.

RADHA: Mahesh, I don't like you smoking and drinking like a mad person.

Mahesh is silent. He doesn't respond and keeps looking at her.

RADHA: Day by day, this habit is only increasing. I thought you'd reduce it.

MAHESH: So, what?

RADHA (angrily): I am allergic to that smell. I am getting a headache. I am not able to sleep with the odour in the room.

Mahesh is again maintaining his silence.

RADHA: I don't think we enjoy our lives.

MAHESH: I have a few more when there is work pressure.

RADHA: Even I am employed. I have work pressure too.

MAHESH: Your pressure is different.

RADHA (furiously): Don't tell me you have more work pressure than what I have! Okay! You don't know what I go through. So, stop comparing.

MAHESH: We are slogging our ass out to get sales.

RADHA: Even we have an ass.

Mahesh looks at her cynically.

RADHA: Don't tell me drinking and smoking are handy solutions to overcome work pressure. Don't bring work as an excuse. There is some other pressure for you.

SCENE 39: INTERIOR, CITADEL SQUARE APARTMENT, MAHESH'S FLAT, LIVING ROOM – MORNING.

*We inter-cut to the living room. Moorthy is seriously reading the newspaper, and Lalitha is engrossed reading the holy book – **The Bhagavad Gita**. The sound of Radha and Mahesh having a heated altercation is audible to Moorthy and Lalitha. They look concerned.*

MOORTHY: There is some fight going on.

Lalitha looks at him and closes the book.

MOORTHY: I know where the problem is?

LALITHA: Where?

MOORTHY: Our son… Mahesh is the root cause.

LALITHA: So, what do we do?

MOORTHY: Better to maintain silence. We'll have peace. Read Gita properly. Lord Krishna will show you the way to have peace.

LALITHA: Lord Krishna says do your duty.

MOORTHY: True. Here we have to keep quiet. That's our duty. Do you understand! Humm!

Lalitha looks at him sorrowfully.

SCENE 40: INTERIOR, CITADEL SQUARE APARTMENT, MAHESH'S FLAT, BEDROOM – MORNING.

We once again intercut to the bedroom. Radha is in an agitated mood with Mahesh. She is furious and standing in front of Mahesh. Mahesh is silently sitting on the chair and looking at Radha's demeanour.

RADHA: Don't think only you handle sales. Even I have a budget of 40 Crores. I am also working day and night to achieve it.

Mahesh does not respond to Radha's rant. He looks like a patient listener. Is it the calm before the storm?

RADHA: Look, Mahesh. I don't think we have a good time together.

MAHESH: You don't seem to enjoy certain things in life.

RADHA: You can be straight on my face. Yes. I am not enjoying bed life with you. We are not having good sex. That's for sure.

MAHESH: You act like a bloody moron.

RADHA (stunned): Hi! Come again!

MAHESH: Yes, you are.

RADHA: Please! Don't use nasty words. Even I know what to say.

MAHESH (furious): Then what?

RADHA (angrily): My body is not a fucking machine to be abused.

MAHESH (sarcastically): I have not used it. Where is the question of abuse? Humm! Instead of hugging you, I can have a wood.

RADHA (agitated): If you want good sex, please go to anyone who can give you. No issues…. Go, have with your sweet Secretary, Stella, who is your sweetheart. She likes you. She will be a better person than me. Go.

Mahesh maintains his silence now as Radha pulls some unwanted stuff out of her emotions. Of course, it was unwarranted, but her inner feelings took over. It looks like she lost control of her mind and vomited it. But somewhere deep in her mind, Radha suspects Mahesh to have some equation with Stella.

RADHA: To be honest, I don't enjoy sex with you. Bloody hell, you have created some kind of an aversion in me. How will I give my body when I am not enjoying it? Sex is divine. You get eternal bliss in the act. With you, I'm developing hatred. I get good feelings when I hug the pillow with a light perfume. But not with you. That's the truth.

Mahesh gets up from the seat. He feels he has had enough from Radha. She has been brutally candid with him about the sexual relationship. It creates a profound impact when a female tells her partner that she is not enjoying sex with him. His manhood has been doubted and questioned now. This is something a male cannot digest easily. A male is like a lion. Mahesh's pride is shattered at the moment, and he somehow has to redeem his pride. Mahesh picks up his cigarette packet and lighter. Then, silently without uttering a word, he goes to the balcony. Radha is watching. Then, she goes to the wardrobe, picks up her dresses, and proceeds to the bathroom.

SCENE 41: INTERIOR, CITADEL SQUARE APARTMENT, MAHESH'S FLAT, LIVING ROOM – MORNING.

It is 8:00 am. Moorthy and Lalitha are silently reading with their mind terribly disturbed. There is calmness in the house after the verbal duel between Radha and Mahesh. Slowly, Mahesh comes into the room with a downcast face. He looks at his mother.

MAHESH: Amma, can you give me a cup of coffee. I will be in the study room.

Lalitha gets up and gives him a gentle stare. She doesn't want to utter any word and goes into the kitchen. Mahesh goes to the fridge, opens it, takes a water bottle, and gulps it. No doubt, it looks like his throat has been parched after the altercation. He goes silently towards the study room again.

SCENE 42: INTERIOR, CITADEL SQUARE APARTMENT, MAHESH'S FLAT, STUDY ROOM – MORNING.

Mahesh is seriously working on his laptop. He scrolls the screen, and the figures of his region pop out. He picks the mobile and,

MAHESH: Stella, good morning. Are you free today?

Mahesh gives a slight pause. His mother brings a cup of filter coffee and places it on the table. She sees him on the call and leaves the room.

MAHESH: Stella, I need your help to create the PPT for my presentation. My mind is a bit disturbed. Not able to concentrate. Day after tomorrow, you know I am leaving for Mumbai.

Mahesh keeps rubbing his forehead. He is upset, and it is clearly showing on his face.

MAHESH: Thanks a lot, Stella. I hope I am not cutting into your Saturday schedule. Okay, I'll come by 10:30 am. After work, we will go out in the evening. Your presence means so much to me. Cheers, honey.

Stella is quite shrewd in understanding her boss. She has to comfort him and offer support when needed. Mahesh badly needs her company now.

SCENE 43: INTERIOR, CITADEL SQUARE APARTMENT, MAHESH'S FLAT, LIVING ROOM – MORNING.

With his hands stretched on the sofa, Moorthy keeps looking at the ceiling. Then, slowly, Lalitha comes from the kitchen and sits next to him. She keeps her right hand on her husband's shoulder gently.

LALITHA: What are you thinking?

MOORTHY: Nothing.

The doorbell rings. Moorthy gets up slowly and proceeds towards the door. Gently opening the door, he surprisingly finds Radha's boss Kishore, with three of his colleagues – Sunitha, Roshan, and Pramodh. Smilingly Moorthy,

MOORTHY: Mr Kishore, so lovely to see you all. Please come in.

KISHORE: Thank you, sir. Just like that, we thought of visiting here.

Moorthy ushers Kishore and his colleagues to the living room. Smilingly, Lalitha gets up.

LALITHA: Great to see you all. After Radha's marriage, this is your second visit to this house.

KISHORE (smilingly): Yes, aunty. Today, we wanted to give Radha a surprise. It was a sudden decision in the morning.

MOORTHY: Just a minute. I'll inform Radha. All of you, please take a seat.

Moorthy proceeds towards Radha's bedroom. He finds the opposite study room door closed. It looks like Mahesh is working inside. Moorthy gently knocks on the bedroom door. From inside, Radha responds.

RADHA: Yes!

MOORTHY: Radha, your boss, Mr. Kishore, has come with three colleagues.

RADHA: Oh! Great. Appa, tell them I'll be in five minutes. Getting dressed.

MOORTHY: Okay, ma.

Moorthy knocks on the door of the study room. Mahesh gently opens.

MOORTHY: Mahesh, Radha's boss, Kishore, has come with three colleagues.

MAHESH: Oh! Okay. Inform Radha.

MOORTHY: I've informed her. You come and meet them.

MAHESH: Appa, you have told me. Just leave it.

Moorthy shakes his head in disbelief. Lalitha is harmoniously discussing with Kishore.

LALITHA: Shall I prepare good fresh filter coffee for you people.

KISHORE: Thanks, aunty. We had it in Sunitha's house. We are going to Muthukaadu boating and Kovalam beach. We wanted to invite Radha and Mahesh if they are free to join.

LALITHA: Oh! That's good. An excellent way to relax on a Saturday.

KISHORE: Yes, aunty. We had too much work last week. So today morning, we decided why not go out and refresh. We didn't inform Radha. It is a sudden plan.

Radha gently comes into the living room gracefully, wearing a ravishingly looking orange churidar, a matching cherry red kameez, and a cherry red – orange dupatta. Her matching ornamental jewellery enhances her beauty further.

RADHA (smilingly): Hey guys! What a surprise to see you all! How is it?

KISHORE: Morning, we decided to go to Muthukadu and Kovalam beach and relax for a while.

RADHA: Oh! That's a fantastic idea.

KISHORE: We thought of inviting you and Mahesh.

RADHA: I thought of going to my mother's place. Anyway, I can come with you guys. No issues. I doubt if Mahesh would come. Well, I'll check. It looks like he is preparing for a meeting in Mumbai.

Radha goes towards the study room and gently taps the door. Mahesh opens. Radha unhurriedly gets in after closing the door slowly.

RADHA: My boss, Kishore, has come with my colleagues. Come and meet them. They are inviting us for a trip to Muthukadu and Kovalam Beach.

MAHESH: You go. I'm not interested. I have important work to complete in the office.

Radha gives him a stare.

RADHA: Your only interest with me is to have sex and only sex. Nothing else.

MAHESH: Radha! Please. I've had enough from you. Just leave me alone. You do anything you want. Please don't spoil my mood.

RADHA: Okay. Fine. I am going to my mother's house after the trip. I will be there for a week or two.

MAHESH: Fair enough. No issues.

RADHA: Okay, meet my colleagues. They want to see you.

Mahesh accompanies Radha to the living room. Kishore comes forward smilingly to meet them and shakes hands with Mahesh.

KISHORE: Hi Mahesh! Good morning.

MAHESH: Good morning, Kishore. Nice to see you all.

KISHORE: How about joining us for a short trip to Muthukadu and Kovalam?

MAHESH: Oh! Thanks for the invite, Kishore. Doing some urgent presentation work. I have a quarterly sales review meeting in Mumbai on Monday. Going to the office after an hour.

KISHORE: Oh! I can understand. Due apologies if we have disturbed you.

MAHESH: No, no. Cool.

Radha sees Kishore.

Radha: I'll get my small suitcase. I'll drop my SUV at my mother's place. From there I'll come with you people.

Radha has, in a way, hinted to her in-laws that she is going to her mother's house. She goes towards her bedroom. After a few minutes, Radha leaves the house with Kishore and her colleagues. Her in-laws are not looking pleased with the developments. Well, they cannot interfere in her personal and professional life. She has the liberty to do anything she wants.

CHAPTER 11

SCENE 44: EXTERIOR, MUTHUKADU BACK WATERS – MORNING

*Kishore gently manoeuvres his Mahindra Scorpio SUV into one of the parking bays abutting the picturesque boating jetty. Colourful boats are stationed on the jetty, with plenty of discerning tourists eager to get in and have a good ride close to the estuary, the meeting point with the mighty Bay of Bengal. Being Saturday, there is a pretty good crowd thronging the ticket counter. Facing the jetty is a sprawling restaurant. The entire area is managed by the Tami Nadu Tourism Development Corporation (TTDC). Muthukadu has become a fantastic tourist destination. Its proximity to the famous port town Mahabalipuram, renowned for its world-famous UNESCO heritage site, **The Shore Temple,** and other heritage monuments, are added attractions. Kishore, Radha, and three colleagues come out of the vehicle. Kishore and Radha look trendy with their coolers and proceed toward the ticket counter. Radha sees Kishore.*

RADHA: Kishore, better I stay back. You people go boating. I have a slight headache.

KISHORE: Why? What happened?

RADHA: I didn't have a good sleep yesterday. If I see water, my headache will increase. I will definitely puke.

Kishore looks at his colleagues.

KISHORE: Sunitha, I suggest you people go for a ride. I will stay back with Radha. Okay.

SUNITHA: Okay, sir.

Sunitha sees Radha.

SUNITHA: Ma'am, sure you cannot make it? It would be great to have you.

RADHA: I have a slight vomiting sensation too. Better, I stay back. I will relax here.

Sunitha, Roshan and Pramodh gently proceed toward the ticket counter. Radha sorrowfully looks at Kishore.

RADHA: Kishore, why not we occupy one of the benches there?

KISHORE: Sure. Come.

They slowly walk down the pathway facing the backwaters and the jetty. Finally, they occupy a corner bench.

KISHORE: Radha, what happened?

Radha doesn't speak a word. Tears begin to drip, and she gently wipes them.

KISHORE: Hey! Radha! What happened. You were okay in the house.

Wiping her tears, Radha keeps her right hand on Kishore's left thigh and looks at him.

RADHA: I had a big fight with Mahesh.

KISHORE: Oh! Shit.

RADHA: I am developing some kind of hatred towards him. He is smoking and drinking like a mad guy. I am so allergic to it. To be honest, I am not enjoying life with him. We hardly romance.

KISHORE: Can't you nicely tell him to decrease it?

RADHA: Tried many times. I have failed miserably. Don't know what his problem is!

KISHORE: So, what is the solution?

RADHA: I think I will go for a divorce soon.

KISHORE (stunned): Radha, are you joking! Humm!

RADHA: Yes, Kishore. I'm serious. The earlier I do better for me. Why drag when it is not going to work?

KISHORE: It is only six months, Radha! You have this kind of thought!

RADHA: I feel that my issues in my personal life are going to screw up my professional life badly. It will ruin me. Do you want that to happen?

Once again, Radha is in tears. She rubs her watery eyes. Kishore feels too sad to see his wonderful colleague in this state. Slowly, he puts his left hand over her shoulders and gently hugs her.

KISHORE: Radha, cool. I can understand your feelings. Give some more time to Mahesh.

RADHA: I have given enough time for him to change. My patience is drained. Many things are working in my mind, Kishore. I'll crystallise it soon before it breaks me to pieces. It is better to nip my problem in the bud stage itself.

Sunitha, Pramodh, and Roshan are coming in a boat towards the jetty. They seem exuberant after having a fantastic 30 minutes ride. Kishore can spot them.

KISHORE: Radha, they are coming. Just refresh your face. We will discuss this later in the evening.

Radha immediately takes a few hand wipes from her bag. She wipes her face gently. Then, wearing the coolers, both get up from their seats to receive them. Radha is concealing her grief, agony, and pain with her coolers.

SCENE 45: INTERIOR, CITADEL SQUARE APARTMENT, MAHESH'S FLAT, LIVING ROOM – MORNING.

Moorthy is watching TIMES NOW English TV news channel seriously. Slowly Lalitha comes and reclines next to him. Looking straight into his eyes.

LALITHA: Did you speak with Mahesh before he left for office.

MOORTHY (gloomily): Yes, I did.

LALITHA (curiously): What did he say?

MOORTHY: He told me to mind my business.

LALITHA: Listening, you kept quiet!

MOORTHY: What do you expect me to do?

LALITHA: You should have told him that things are not looking good.

MOORTHY: Yes. I did. He is pointing fingers at us now. He feels that we are the root cause.

LALITHA (surprised): In what way we are responsible?

MOORTHY: We didn't endorse him marrying Stella. Moreover, he had Sevvai dhosham. In a way, he is right. We are responsible to some extent.

LALITHA (furiously): Have you gone mad or what? How can you have a Christian daughter-in-law in the house?

MOORTHY (angrily): In what way it is wrong? Stella is a very good person. What if she is a Christian! Humm! I was okay with it. Only you and your family members objected. Your bloody brothers were adamant. You listen to them more than what your husband says! Now that anger in Mahesh is showing colours differently. Mind you, Stella helped him in many ways.

LALITHA: Oh! I like it. Now, you are blaming my family.

MOORTHY: Look! Radha is a fantastic and highly brilliant person. No second thoughts about it. We should be blessed to have her as our daughter-in-law. Our son is gifted to have her as his wife. But she is not the ideal person for Mahesh. They are poles apart. Now, I get a feeling their professional egos are going to clash more and more. It is going to tear them apart.

LALITHA: So, what do we do?

MOORTHY: If we broach the topic again with Mahesh, we will be forced to leave the house. That will be our plight! Do you want that to happen?

Lalitha gives her husband a good stare. She gets up slowly and leaves for the kitchen, murmuring. Annoyed, Moorthy looks at her.

MOORTHY: Tell straight on my face if you want to say something. Don't murmur. It's a dirty disease with you.

Moorthy once again watches the television in a disillusioned mood. Watching the TV, he keeps murmuring now. Lalitha slightly peeps through the kitchen entrance and looks at him sarcastically.

LALITHA: Why are you murmuring now? Watch TV properly.

MOORTHY: Your disease is a contagious one. Got infected through you.

SCENE 46: INTERIOR, JOE & SHAN LTD, OFFICE – MORNING

Stella is inside Mahesh's cabin, smartly dressed in her cream corduroy jeans and a checked half-sleeve cotton short. She looks elegant and does serious presentation work on the laptop computer. The jasmine flower bunch pinned to her tresses lifts her outlook to a different level. She is engrossed in bringing the graphical representation of the sales figure of the southern region. Mahesh opens the door and comes in gently. Standing near Stella, he looks at the graph. Stella looks at him gently with a seducing smile.

STELLA: What, Marlboro man! Went to the terrace to enjoy a good fag!

MAHESH: Oh! Yeah. Just wanted to relax a bit and take some fresh air.

STELLA: Have four more slides to complete.

MAHESH: The graph looks pretty good.

STELLA: Your sales figures are impressive. The graph has to look good only! Mark my word, you will floor the senior management with your presentation.

Hearing the soothing compliments, Mahesh is rejuvenated and slowly puts his two hands around Stella's cheek and strokes it gently.

MAHESH: Stella, you are so sweet, dear. Your words are lifting my spirits.

STELLA (sarcastically): Lifting only spirits!

MAHESH: Many things.

Stella gives him a cute look. Mahesh is slowly rubbing her frontal neck area.

STELLA: Mahi, watch out. The door is open.

MAHESH: Don't worry. I have put the latch. No one has come to the office yet. RPMs (Regional Product Managers) are expected after 1:00 pm only.

STELLA (softly): Mahi, are you not feeling bad having a relationship with me when you have Radha? I know I have corrupted you and myself. You dragged me into this relationship somehow. Blindly, I fell. Don't know how to come out now. Even I need it knowing pretty well it is wrong.

MAHESH: Stella, I don't have a choice. Dear, I need you badly in my life. I'll be finished if you are not there.

Mahesh lifts her head upwards, facing his face.

MAHESH: You want to see your Mahesh happy! Humm!

Stella slowly removes his hands and looks at the laptop screen.

STELLA: Okay, Mahi, allow me to complete. Evening you can play, dear. I'm there for you.

MAHESH: Your mother is there!

STELLA: No. She is expected next month. From Bangalore, she went to Goa to stay with her brother's family.

MAHESH: Okay, you finish the presentation. I am not going to disturb you.

Mahesh gives a sweet lighting kiss on her cheek. Stella delicately stares at him.

STELLA: Happy! Satisfied! Now, do your work.

Mahesh slowly opens the door latch and goes out again. He goes to the coffee vending machine and fills two cups. Gradually he comes back to his cabin and sees Stella.

MAHESH: Here, sweetie.

STELLA: Oh! So sweet of you. I wanted it badly. Thanks, dear.

Mahesh takes his seat and relishes the coffee. The romantic chemistry between Mahesh and Stella is definitely going strong. Today, Mahesh wants to be close with Stella after Radha's outburst and unwanted comments. Mahesh feels badly wounded in his mind. For him, Stella is an excellent consoling factor and stress reliever in many ways. He has to relieve his agony and pain only through Stella. However, will this kind of relationship sustain and for how long? Is it moral for Mahesh to have a relationship with two females? Infidelity exists in society, and we attribute so many reasons to it. In this contemporary world, extramarital affairs and other relationships are increasing rapidly – courtesy of the complex changing dynamics in this fast world. Only time will give an appropriate answer to many unresolved issues between Mahesh and Radha.

CHAPTER 12

Radha's father, Natarajan, expired, succumbing to his metastatic cancer. Radha relocates to her parent's house to be with her mother and her maternal aunt and uncle, who have shifted from Bangalore. Since Radha has a troubled marital life, she has used her father's demise to move out of her in-law's house. Blessing in disguise, it has come in handy. At least Radha has some bliss now staying with her wonderful mother and her relatives. On the other hand, Mahesh is also relieved that his wife is not there. It has given him an excellent opportunity to enhance his romantic exploits with his sweetheart, Stella.

SCENE 47: INTERIOR, HIGH TECH GLOBAL HEALTHCARE SOLUTIONS, CONFERENCE HALL – AFTERNOON

The executives of the Chennai region have assembled in the conference room smartly dressed in their official full suits. They are all looking anxious and eager. Radha is conversing slowly with Kishore. Suddenly the door opens, and Raghav, the Regional Director, ushers Sunil Tandon, the company's President. The people in the hall get up as a mark of respect. Sunil, with a pleasing smile, takes centre stage.

SUNIL TANDON: My dear colleagues and the incredible Chennai team. Good morning.

The team reciprocate his good wishes delightfully.

SUNIL TANDON: Friends, we value the excellent contributions made by our employees. Our policy encourages and motivates people to excel and take pride in their job. But, equally, their association with the organization should also give them a good social status.

The team is looking enthusiastic about listening to Sunil. He has kindled their interests, and the excitement is looming on their faces.

SUNIL TANDON: Given our future growth opportunities and expansion of our businesses, I am happy to announce the elevation of Mr. Raghav as the Country Head for emerging markets.

Raghav gently gets up, acknowledges and reciprocates his thankful gesture to Sunil.

SUNIL TANDON: Next, I am happy to announce Mr. Kishore as the Executive Director, Asia Pacific region. We will also set up a regional office in Singapore. Kishore will oversee all verticals in the healthcare business.

Kishore exuberantly gets up from his seat and acknowledges. His colleagues applaud, listening to the great news.

SUNIL TANDON: Now, it is my great pleasure to announce the elevation of our charming beauty, Mrs. Radha, as the Vice President of the Asia-Pacific region for the complete range of our hospital-related software applications. This organization believes in equal opportunities, and Radha will be the first female to head such a vast region. Radha, through her team, has proved her skill in developing excellent products for our customers.

Radha blissfully gets up, and with folded hands, she thanks Sunil for the honour. She is ecstatic, and Kishore gently pats her back. The team members give her thunderous applause. They are excited about the elevation. All of them feel it is an excellent move by the management.

SUNIL TANDON: Kishore, use our Chennai facility until you set up the office in Singapore. Our good customer, Park & Castle Group, has offered us an entire six thousand square feet floor in their prestigious headquarters building. So, you can shift a few people from the Chennai office. Well, You and Radha work out the modalities.

KISHORE: Sure. I'll work it out with Radha.

SUNIL TANDON: Friends, other promotions, I've approved based on your recommendations. I hope it will create a pleasant atmosphere for people to excel and scale greater heights. Okay, we will break for lunch now. Evening we are having a party.

SCENE 48: INTERIOR, HIGH TECH GLOBAL HEALTHCARE SOLUTIONS, RADHA'S CABIN – AFTERNOON

Radha is in her room looking at the computer screen. A few bouquets are placed on top of the shelf behind her. Her colleagues have gifted her after hearing the news of her elevation as Vice President. Indeed, a proud moment to cherish and a motivation for them to perform. Likewise, many of her team members have been rewarded with good promotions. Radha picks up her mobile and dials.

RADHA: Mahesh, I just want to convey one good news. Where are you?

Intercut with Mahesh.

MAHESH: I'm in Trivandrum. What good news?

RADHA: I have been promoted as Vice President of the Asia-Pacific region.

MAHESH: Oh! Okay. Congrats. Anything else!

RADHA: Well, we are setting up the regional office in Singapore. I'll be spending at least a week to ten days there. Next week, I'm going to Singapore.

MAHESH: Okay. Fine. Thanks for the info.

RADHA: The way you respond, you look like a lifeless creature.

MAHESH: You can say anything you want. No issues. Anyway, you are known to make big statements! This is because you have a unique trait.

RADHA: Mahesh, I want to tell you another important aspect.

MAHESH: What? Can you make it fast? Need to attend a meeting.

RADHA: Mahesh, I want a mutual consent divorce. I want to end our marriage. I'm not interested in leading my life with you anymore. I'm sorry. The earlier I do; it is better for us.

MAHESH: Have you made up your mind firm?

RADHA: Yes. I have given enough thought to it for a while. I don't think I'm the right person for you. I don't think both of us are compatible with each other. So let us not have any issues with our separation. Let us shake hands and part amicably.

MAHESH: Okay. Let's put our papers to the family court if that's your wish. No issues.

Mahesh exhibits some sense of maturity rather than entering into unwanted arguments with Radha. It is not going to cut any ice with her. Radha's opening on the divorce could be construed as a new beginning for Mahesh. A sign of a new dawn for him in many ways. Now, Mahesh is like a free bird and has the freedom to do things without any inhibitions. So is Radha. She has unfettered liberty and is not encapsulated. So, what if the marriage breaks? In this contemporary world, these things have become common. People find greener pastures to embark on and move on with life. Only a tiny spark is needed today to break a relationship. People don't have the patience to reconcile and resolve issues in this jet-speed world.

RADHA: I will make one more visit to your house to take my things. Please inform your parents.

MAHESH: Okay, fine. As per your wish, you go ahead. I'm back after a week only.

RADHA: My good wishes to you, Mahesh, for all success in your endeavours.

MAHESH: Okay, good wishes to you too.

SCENE 49: INTERIOR, HIGH TECH GLOBAL HEALTHCARE SOLUTIONS, KISHORE'S CABIN – AFTERNOON

Radha slowly comes and knocks on the cabin door. Gently opening the door, she takes the seat opposite Kishore. She has some new radiation flowing from her face.

KISHORE: What, Radha? You seem rejuvenated. Looks like you are in high spirits!

RADHA: Yes. In a way. My spirits are sky-high. I have touched Mount Everest.

KISHORE: Ha! That's great. The promotion has done wonders, it looks like!

RADHA: Absolutely. Had a chat with Mahesh. He is in Trivandrum.

KISHORE: Conveyed your promotion to him?

RADHA: Yes. He was like a moron! He only acknowledged with simple congrats.

KISHORE: Is he not happy with his wife getting a good promotion.

RADHA (sarcastically): More than that, he was happy with my other announcement.

KISHORE: What announcement?

RADHA: Said to him that we will part ways and that I seek mutual consent divorce.

KISHORE (stunned): What! Are you serious?

RADHA: Yes. Kishore. Made my mind firm. Well, this week, I'll make one last visit to his house as a daughter-in-law to pack my things. That's it. My mind is free.

KISHORE: Has he agreed?

RADHA: Yes. Inwardly he is exuberant. Probably no more of my torture, I guess.

KISHORE: Oh! Shit. So, what are you going to do?

RADHA: Many things are revolving in my mind. I'll discuss this with you during our Singapore trip. But, mark my word, you'll see a different Radha after we return.

Radha gently places her right hand on Kishore's hand with tears trickling. Kishore looks at her without winking his eyes.

RADHA: Kishore, can I seek your help for many things in my life?

Kishore reciprocates by placing his right hand on Radha's hand. He looks at her sorrowfully. Now, Radha has created some suspense in Kishore's mind. She is not revealing it explicitly. However, he is magnanimous not to probe further.

KISHORE: Radha, you can count on me. I'll be there for you. Don't worry.

RADHA: Thank you so much, Kishore. I value your relationship.

CHAPTER 13

SCENE 50: INTERIOR, CITADEL SQUARE APARTMENT, MAHESH'S FLAT – EVENING

Radha is waiting outside the flat door along with her friend, Rohini. This visit would be the last to her in-law's house. She has come to collect her belongings. The door opens, and Mahesh's parents, Moorthy and Lalitha, look at Radha with sad faces. They are disturbed by the developments.

MOORTHY: Radha, please come in.

Radha and Rohini gently enter the living room. Radha looks at her in-laws gloomily.

RADHA: Sorry, Appa. I didn't have a choice. It is better for both of us.

MOORTHY (Sadly): Radhama, I don't want to say anything. We are feeling bad that you are leaving us. We are not fortunate to have you as our daughter-in-law.

Radha is not keen to prolong the conversation, as it would leave bad tastes on both sides. She is an intelligent lady.

RADHA: Appa, I'll go to my room and take my items with your permission.

MOORTHY: Okay, ma. Please carry on. Let me know if you need any help.

RADHA: Thanks, pa.

SCENE 51: INTERIOR, CITADEL SQUARE APARTMENT, MAHESH'S FLAT, BEDROOM – EVENING

Radha is clearing all her dress materials from the wardrobe, and Rohini is keeping them on the bed in an orderly manner. Radha now brings the foldable ladder from the storeroom. She needs the suitcases kept in the loft cupboard. Rohini watches Radha unfolding the ladder and placing it just beneath the loft. She climbs slowly.

ROHINI: Ma'am, be careful. Shall I hold the ladder?

RADHA: The ladder is a good one. Pretty Steady. Okay, I'll give you the suitcases. You keep it on the bed.

ROHINI: Okay, ma'am.

Radha is cautiously climbing the ladder to reach the loft door. Rohini is seriously looking at her without winking her eyes. Radha takes a big, burgundy American Tourister soft luggage suitcase and gives it to Rohini. Now, Radha climbs to the top step of the ladder to have a good view and accessibility of the loft. As she pulls out another big suitcase, a big plastic cover falls from the loft. Rohini, with fear, looks at Radha.

ROHINI: Ma'am, be careful. I'll hold the suitcase.

Radha gently gives the suitcase to Rohini.

RADHA: Rohini, give me the cover.

Rohini takes the fallen cover from the floor and hands it over to Radha. Radha carefully takes the papers from inside, standing on top of the ladder. Then, looking stunned, she murmurs.

RADHA: Medical report from Dr.Samuel Joseph, Chief Consultant Psychiatrist, SJ hospital!

Radha glances at a few pages of the report and again murmurs, reading the final summary.

RADHA: Manic Depressive Psychosis, mild mood disorder due to emotional disturbances!

Radha is stunned by reading the report. She opens another cover and finds many greeting cards from Stella. Radha again glances through the cards. Closing her eyes with two hands, Radha is in deep thoughts. Rohini is curiously watching in silence. She knows that something has disturbed Radha. Removing her hands from the face, Radha looks at Rohini.

RADHA: Rohini, if you don't mind, can I have my mobile? It is there in my shoulder bag.

ROHINI: Sure, ma'am.

Rohini takes the mobile from the bag and hands it to Radha inquisitively. Standing on one leg of the ladder, Radha places the medical report on the resting pad of the ladder. She takes a few pictures of the medical papers and other cards. She puts all the items back into the same cover and places them deep inside the loft. Rohini is silently watching the developments. Radha climbs down the ladder and folds it. Placing the ladder in one corner of the room, Radha proceeds to the main wardrobe, takes all her garments, and puts it on the bed. She looks at Rohini.

RADHA: Rohini, all sarees, you keep them in the blue American Tourister suitcase. Rest of the items, I'll pack them in the other two suitcases.

ROHINI (Obediently): Yes, ma'am.

As Radha and Rohini pack the items, someone from outside gently knocks on the door. Radha looks towards the door.

RADHA: Yes, coming. Please wait.

Opening the door, Radha finds her mother-in-law standing with a tray containing two cups of pure filter coffee and biscuits. The aroma diffuses in the air.

RADHA (stunned): Amma, why all this trouble?

LALITHA (tearfully): It's okay, ma. Please have. Today will be the last day I will serve you as your mother-in-law.

RADHA: Amma, I can still be a good friend to you and Appa. Our relationship will not get cut just because I am walking out of the family.

LALITHA (emotionally): Thanks, ma. Any time you can come to this house. Treat this as your house.

Radha humbly takes the tray. Wiping the eyes with her saree pallu, Lalitha leaves the room. Radha offers a cup to Rohini.

ROHINI: Excellent taste! The aroma stays in the throat.

RADHA: Amma is good at making pure filter coffee. She knows that I relish it.

SCENE 52: INTERIOR, CITADEL SQUARE APARTMENT, MAHESH'S FLAT, LIVING ROOM – EVENING

Moorthy and Lalitha look tearfully sober and wait for Radha to emerge from the bedroom. Slowly Radha and Rohini enter the hall with three big suitcases and two carton boxes. Moorthy and Lalitha gently get up from the sofa. Moorthy has a small artistically crafted wooden box. He looks at her emotionally.

MOORTHY: Radha, these are your jewels. I have taken it from the locker. Just check it.

Radha silently receives it and looks at her in-laws regretfully.

RADHA: Thanks, pa. Sorry for our separation. I think it is all for good. I know Mahesh will see a new life from now on.

Radha looks at Rohini.

RADHA: Rohini, give me the jewel box.

Rohini, as directed, hands over a flat jewel box. Radha looks at her in-laws.

RADHA: Appa, this is my Mangalsuthra. Please have it.

Moorthy receives it gently. Lalitha weeps profusely, seeing the act. Radha gently goes forward and hugs her. In her low tone,

RADHA: Amma, I am leaving this house with your blessings. I value that. You are, in a way, like my mother.

Lalitha looks at Radha tearfully.

LALITHA: Radhama, I apologise if I have spoken harsh words against you. Please don't keep anything in your mind.

RADHA: Sure, ma... Okay, it is time for me to leave.

Radha slowly bends down and prostrates before her in-laws for one last time. Moorthy and Lalitha place their hands on Radha's head symbolically.

MOORTHY: Our blessings are always with you. May you shine brilliantly in your personal and professional life. Keep in touch.

RADHA: Sure, pa

CHAPTER 14

SCENE 53: INTERIOR, RIVER VIEW APARTMENT, RADHA'S FLAT, BEDROOM – EVENING

Radha, wearing a trendy cool cotton beige gown, is casually resting on her bed and seriously dialling her mobile. She gets through the connection with a blissful smile.

RADHA: Is it Dr.Amita!... (*after a pause*) Hi, Amita! How are you? How is your practice going?

Radha is giving a patient listening with a smile.

RADHA: Amita, listen, I want to discuss a personal medical issue.

After a slight pause

RADHA: Amita, my relationship with my husband, is over. Well, things didn't work between us. Last week, we split. We were going for a mutual consent divorce. Happen to bounce on his medical report and love letters when I tried to remove my suitcases from the loft.

Once again, Radha gives a patient listening.

RADHA: I feel he is having an affair with his Secretary, Stella. I don't understand why he didn't settle with her! She is a cute-looking female with good sharp features.

After a pause

RADHA: The medical report's final diagnosis reveals 'Manic Depressive Psychosis, mild mood disorder due to emotional disturbances.'

Without winking her eyes, Radha looks at the ceiling. She is engrossed in the response from Amita. It seems like Amita is enlightening Radha with vital knowledge. But is it going to help her in any way? Only time will tell!

RADHA: Thanks a lot, Amita, for explaining. Appreciate it. Okay, listen, I am going to Singapore the day after tomorrow and will be back after a fortnight. We will catch up. You are most welcome to my house. My mother will be immensely pleased to see you. Okay, take care.

Radha keeps the mobile on the small lamp table by the bed and looks at the ceiling. Well, something is disturbing her mind now as her eyes look watery. Radha gently wipes her tears. Why has Radha suddenly become this emotional after conversing with Dr. Amita? Don't know! Slowly, she pulls her blanket over her and rests sideways in the sea of tranquillity.

SCENE 54: EXTERIOR, SPENCER PLAZA MALL – NEXT DAY AFTERNOON.

The iconic huge modern Spencer Mall looks majestic, with a crowd thronging the main entrance. Once upon a time, the vintage classic British building of Indo-Saracenic architecture stood in this place. When constructed in 1895, The Spencer was the first mall and departmental store in the country and probably in South Asia. Unfortunately, the old heritage building got destroyed in a fire accident on February 13, 1981. As a result, a modern multi-storeyed mall cum office structure came at the same site.

Jubilantly holding two big bags, Radha emerges from the main entrance. She proceeds towards her SUV. She has made some excellent purchases of branded dress materials before leaving for a two weeks official tour to Singapore along with Kishore. As she is about to drive out of the parking bay, she notices Mahesh gently hugging Stella at her back and both of them entering the mall. She is stunned for a moment and keeps looking at them. Finally, Radha switches off the engine and tears begin to flow. She closes her eyes with her right thumb and index finger for a few seconds. Weird things seem to be striking her mind. Regaining her composure, gently Radha wipes her tears. Cranking the engine again, Radha smoothly drives away from the sprawling campus.

SCENE 55: INTERIOR, RIVER VIEW APARTMENT, RADHA'S FLAT, BEDROOM – EVENING

Radha, wearing a pink colour nightie, is walking restlessly up and down in her bedroom. After seeing Mahesh with Stella at the Spencer Mall, something is disturbing her mind. Slowly, she picks up her mobile and dials it. Finally, she gets the connection through.

RADHA: Hi Stella! How are you?

Radha is looking through the balcony door.

RADHA: Stella, just like that, felt like talking with you. I hope I have not disturbed you, I guess.

Radha is patiently listening to the response from Stella. Then, intercut with Stella, who is reclining on the bed in her house.

Stella is looking cute with her below-knee skirt and a matching T-shirt.

STELLA: So sweet of you to think of me, Radha. You are a wonderful person.

RADHA: Stella, can I have a personal chat with you? I hope no one is around you!

STELLA: No issues, Radha. You are most welcome. I respect you a lot.

RADHA: Thank you, Stella. Okay, I want to catch up with you after a fortnight. I want to discuss with you something very personal.

STELLA (stunned): Anything disturbing you, Radha. You can discuss it now if you want. I'm okay with it.

RADHA: No, Stella. Not today. I'm not in the right frame of my mind. You know why! Presume Mahesh would have told you. Tomorrow, I am leaving for Singapore for two weeks official visit. I don't want my mind to be disturbed. I hope you'll understand.

STELLA: I feel sad after what I heard from Mahesh. I can understand your feelings, Radha. Take it from me; God will show you some bright light to cherish.

RADHA: Humble request, Stella. I don't want Mahesh to know that I chatted with you. You promise me that you'll not divulge.

STELLA: Radha, you can trust me. I'll not tell Mahesh. I promise.

RADHA: Thank you, dear. I appreciate it. After I land in Chennai, I'll give you a call. We can catch up for lunch or dinner at Spencer's Food Court or somewhere near us. Is it okay?

Radha mentioning Spencer Mall kindles Stella's mind. However, Stella is unruffled and is not keen to probe. Being a shrewd female, she is playing it safe. She is not eager to discuss the divorce issue between Radha and Mahesh and feels this is not the ideal time. Undoubtedly, Stella is also caught in a whirlpool situation. Radha is also behaving diplomatically with her, so why stir up unnecessarily?

STELLA: No issues, Radha. We will catch up. Feel free to talk with me anytime. I'm your good friend. Okay.

RADHA: God bless you, dear. You'll always remain my good friend.

STELLA: Sweetie, have a pleasant and safe journey. Just keep your mind calm.

RADHA: Thank you so much. Cheers baby.

Radha keeps the mobile on her table. She stretches her hands as if she is highly relieved. From the small refrigerator beneath her TV set, Radha opens the door and takes a tetra pack of apple juice. She goes to the balcony and gently sucks the juice admiring the serene beauty of Chennai city and the Adyar river nearby.

CHAPTER 15

SCENE 56: INTERIOR, HIGH TECH GLOBAL HEALTHCARE SOLUTIONS – MORNING

Radha and Kishore have just returned from a fruitful trip to Singapore. Within a short period, they established the Asia-Pacific regional office there. In the coming months, Radha and Kishore will be relocating to Singapore. There is a new awakening within Radha. A new ray of hope to treasure.

Radha, wearing trendy beige colour pants and a matching brown with yellow striped formal full sleeve shirt, is coming out of her cabin looking exuberant. She waves her right hand to a few colleagues in the big hall smilingly. Then, she proceeds toward Kishore's cabin and knocks on the door gently. From inside, there is a soft, pleasant voice.

KISHORE: Come in.

Radha gracefully enters the room and sees Kishore typing a letter. He looks up and sees her smilingly.

KISHORE: Hi! Take a seat. Just give me a minute.

RADHA: Sure.

Kishore seriously looks at the laptop screen blissfully. He looks at Radha.

KISHORE: Sent our project proposal to Sunil. I'm confident he'll give his approval. You have done an excellent presentation. Moreover, you are his pet.

RADHA: You are my pillar of strength. When you are there, I can handle things confidently.

KISHORE: Want to discuss something?

RADHA: Yes. Something very personal.

KISHORE (curiously): Personal!

RADHA: I need your help.

KISHORE: Radha, my help is always there for you. You don't have to ask for it.

RADHA: Can you make yourself free this evening? I would like you to accompany me to a special place.

KISHORE (inquisitively): Where?

RADHA: To Holy & Sacred Home

KISHORE: What work do you have there?

RADHA: Kishore, you will see a new Radha from today onwards. Radha is going to see a new world and a new horizon.

KISHORE (surprisingly): Not able to get you. You sound poetic. Talk straight, dear.

RADHA: Did I not tell you in Singapore that you'll find Radha a changed person after arriving in Chennai?

KISHORE: You hinted but didn't elaborate. Okay, tell me what it is.

RADHA: I want to do something meaningful in my life after all I went through.

KISHORE: I can't understand.

RADHA: I have decided one thing firm – no more marriage in my life. No way. I've buried the concept of Sevvai dhosham and divorce in my mind. I don't even want to think of these words.

For a few seconds, the words of Radha shake Kishore's mind. It is like a thunderbolt on his head. What is Radha trying to convey? She sounds circumspect. Why is she beating around the bush instead of opening it clear with Kishore?

KISHORE (patiently): Okay, what are you going to do?

RADHA: Kishore, you'll see for yourself once you visit the place.

KISHORE: Why so much suspense, Radha? Why can't you be open?

RADHA: Well, Kishore. What I am going to do, you may like or dislike. But I'm firm in my thoughts. It looks like God is showing me a bright ray of light in my life. So, I need to absorb that light and move on to have peace and prosperity.

KISHORE: No doubt, I see a distinct change in your attitude and behaviour since you broke up with Mahesh. Well, you are an intelligent lady. Radha, I offer my good wishes to you.

RADHA: Thank you, Kishore.

KISHORE: Presume your family is aware of your move?

RADHA: Yes. I conveyed my thoughts to my mother and aunty the day before yesterday. They have welcomed my interest. They don't have a choice other than to accept it. Well, today, you'll definitely come to know.

KISHORE (diplomatically): Okay. Cool. What time do we leave?

RADHA: 5:30 pm. Is it okay?

KISHORE: Okay. Fine. I'll be ready.

SCENE 57: EXTERIOR, HOLY & SACRED HOME – EVENING

It is 6:15 pm. Radha's SUV, followed by Kishore's SUV, gently come and stop before the main gate. Radha honks a few times. The security staff opens the big gate for the SUVs to enter. Many children are playing joyfully in the open yard. Many children have already surrounded their vehicle as Radha and Kishore come out of the SUV. It looks like Radha is a well-known person on the campus, and children recognise her. Carrying a big cloth bag, Radha smilingly looks at the children. A few come and hug her and catch her hands. Kishore is silently in awe, looking at the reception accorded.

CHILDREN: Good evening, aunty. Good evening, aunty.

Radha gently reciprocates their greetings.

RADHA: Good evening, sweeties. Please go and play. I'll meet you all later. Okay.

Listening to her command, the children leave the parking area and continue to enjoy their games. Kishore, in admiration, looks at Radha.

KISHORE: Sprawling campus. It looks like the children are so attached to you.

RADHA: This home is doing a yeomen service to people. Very dedicated and committed to the cause. Rare to find. Close to 200 students are staying in this home with good facilities. Holy & Sacred Convent is the adjacent campus.

KISHORE: I can see it. Beautiful campus. I know you are an alumnus of the school.

A lady staff member in her mid-forties wearing a white sari comes near Radha.

STAFF: Madam, Sister Angela is in her room. She said you are coming. Please come, madam.

RADHA: Oh! So nice of her.

Radha looks at Kishore. He is clueless about his presence on this campus. Is she going to spring some surprise?

RADHA: Kishore, come.

SCENE 58: INTERIOR, HOLY & SACRED HOME – EVENING

The staff member ushers Radha and Kishore into the main building. As they keep walking down the wide corridor, a few sisters wearing the traditional white Christian robes pass by. Smilingly, they wave their hands at Radha, and she acknowledges. Next, the staff invites them to the main hall leading to the room of Sister (Sr.) Angela, the home's Chief Warden and former Principal of the convent. First, the staff peeps through a small window on the door to see if anyone is in the room. Then, she turns back and looks at Radha.

STAFF: Sr.Angela is talking with Sr.Jennifer. Just wait, I'll inform Sr.Angela. Please take a seat.

RADHA: Sure. Thank you, sister.

The staff gently knocks on the door and enters. After a few seconds, Sr.Angela and Sr.Jennifer come out of the room looking for Radha. Looking at them, Radha gets up blissfully, and Kishore follows.

Sr.ANGELA: Hello, dear. Welcome to our home. So lovely to see you.

Both Sisters hug Radha warmly to shower their love and affection. Radha looks at them.

RADHA: Sister, this is my guest, Kishore. He is my boss, Executive Director of the Asia Pacific region. Sister, Kishore is more than a boss to me. He is like my family member.

Sr.ANGELA: Welcome, Mr. Kishore. Radha used to be my brilliant student in school. A topper and a Tamil Nadu State rank holder. She is so much associated with the school and this home. Radha is an asset to us.

KISHORE: Sister, this is my first visit to this campus. I am aware that Radha is doing some work here. Today, she was keen that I should accompany her.

Sr.ANGELA: Radha has a great mind and heart to do noble deeds. Both of you, please come.

SCENE 59: INTERIOR, HOLY & SACRED HOME, Sr.ANGELA'S ROOM – EVENING

Kishore and Radha take seats opposite Sr.Angela. Sr.Angela looks at Sr. Jennifer.

Sr.ANGELA: Jennifer, tell Daphne madam Radha has come to invite them. Let her bring her grandchildren Vincent and Melinda.

Sr.JENNIFER: Sure, sister. I'll bring them.

Sr.Jennifer leaves the room. Sr Angela looks at Radha.

Sr.ANGELA: Radha. God will be with you always. You have shown great wisdom in taking the family with you. Did you inform Mr. Kishore?

RADHA: No, sister.

Kishore is looking bewildered. He looks at Sr. Angela without winking his eyes.

Sr.ANGELA (softly): Mr. Kishore, we have two cute children, Vincent and Melinda. They lost their parents in a car accident on the Dharmapuri – Salem highway two years ago. Their car had a collision with a lorry coming in the opposite direction. Both died on the spot. Like you people, both of them were IT professionals. Wonderful couples. The children didn't have relatives to take care of them. So, we took them in our care along with their grandmother. Now, Radha has come forward to give them a new life. She will be an excellent guardian to them. The children are very fond of her.

Listening to the words of Sr.Angela, Kishore has tears flowing. He places his right hand on Radha's hand.

KISHORE: Radha, I feel so proud of you. My God! You are a role model for me to lead my life. What a noble deed you have exhibited!

Wiping his teary eyes, Kishore pats Radha. Sr.Jennifer arrives with Daphne and her grandchildren. Vincent and Melinda blissfully hug Radha.

Sr.ANGELA: Daphne, your time has come to go to Radha's home. Enjoy the rest of your life with her family. She will be a fantastic guardian to you people. Vincent and Melinda will have a great future through her loving care. Okay!

DAPHNE: Thank you so much, sister, for all help rendered. We will never forget you in our lives. When I see Radha madam, I feel like seeing my daughter, Nancy.

Sr.ANGELA: Daphne, the Lord has shown you and your children a wonderful person. The Lord has blessed you people in many ways. You cannot have any better person than Radha. Enjoy your life with her family.

Sr.Angela looks at Radha.

Sr.ANGELA: Radha, today we had a small farewell party for the children on our campus. They are looking excited to be with you.

RADHA: Sister, I promise you before the Lord. They will lead a good life under my care.

SCENE 60: EXTERIOR, HOLY & SACRED HOME, PARKING AREA – EVENING

Radha is loading the belongings of Daphne and her grandchildren into the dickey area of her SUV. Kishore is helping her. Sr.Angela and other staff members are there to bid farewell. Radha sees Sr.Angela.

RADHA: Sister, we will take leave. Thank you so much for the help.

Sr.ANGELA: We need to thank you for the noble gesture. Keep coming to home and school. We need people like you. Bring Mr.Kishore often.

RADHA: Sure, sister. How can I forget you all?

Radha opens the back door for Daphne and her grandchildren to enter. A few children assembled nearby wave their hands. Then, slowly, Radha goes near Kishore, who is organising the baggage properly in the dickey.

RADHA: Kishore, could you please come to my house? Have dinner. My mother is preparing a special dinner today. Come.

KISHORE: You feel I should come?

RADHA: Yes. You should. My mother will feel so happy to see you.

KISHORE (hesitantly): Okay. Radha, even I want to have some personal discussion with you. I want to share my mind with you. You have opened my eyes today to a different world.

RADHA: Oh! Sure. I, too, have thoughts to be shared with you.

Kishore enters his SUV. Sr.Angela and other staff wave their hands at the departing vehicles.

CHAPTER 16

SCENE 61: INTERIOR, SPENCER MALL, FOOD COURT – AFTERNOON

In the sprawling-food court dotted with numerous restaurants to satisfy the appetite of discerning customers, Radha has occupied the corner table along with Daphne, Vincent and Melinda. The children are enjoying the Mexican Delight Pizza and looking excited. They are about to finish and look at Radha.

RADHA (smilingly): Sweeties, I am getting ice cream. Okay! After some time, both of you enjoy the play area. Happy!

The children nod their heads in the affirmative. A smart-looking waitress holding a tray with both hands brings the cups of Tutti Frutti ice cream. She gently serves them.

RADHA: Have ice cream slowly. Don't spill on your shirt. Okay.

The children endorse her request. From a distance, the gorgeous-looking Stella, wearing a fashionable weekend outfit of light blue jeans and dark blue knitted full-sleeve T-shirt, approaches Radha. Radha waves her hand. Radha is fulfilling the date she committed with Stella before her departure to Singapore. Stella comes and gently hugs Radha.

STELLA: Nice to see you, Radha. It looks like you have come with guests. How was your trip to Singapore?

RADHA: The trip was great. Stella, meet Daphne aunty, Vincent, and Melinda.

STELLA: Oh! These children are so sweet and cute.

Stella goes near them and gives them a sweet kiss. Later, she occupies a seat opposite Radha.

RADHA: Stella, these people are part of my family.

STELLA (surprised): Your family!

RADHA: Yes. I am their guardian. Very soon, I will adopt the children.

STELLA: I don't get you.

Radha sees the children seriously engrossed in eating the ice cream.

RADHA (softly): These lovely children lost their parents in a car accident two years ago. Holy & Sacred Home took them under their care.

STELLA: Oh! So sad.

RADHA: I have known the Home and the Convent for many years. I'm closely associated. I am an alumnus of the Holy & Sacred Convent. After my break-up with Mahesh, I decided to do something purposeful and meaningful in my life. So, I decided to be their guardian. They moved into my house yesterday along with their grandmother, Daphne.

Stella becomes emotional, listening with watery eyes.

STELLA: Radha, you brought tears from my eyes. My God! I see real God through you. I want to hug and kiss you.

Stella, moved by her emotions, gets up and gently hugs Radha with a kiss. Then, wiping her eyes, she retakes the seat. The children have finished relishing the ice cream. Radha looks at them.

RADHA: Both of you want to enjoy some time in that play area. Humm!

The little ones shake their head, endorsing her thoughts.

RADHA: Daphne aunty. You can take them to the play area there. Let them spend some time. I'll be with my friend, Stella.

Daphne takes her grandchildren towards the tiny tots' play area nearby.

STELLA: Radha, I am searching for words to express my feelings. I pray Lord to shower enormous blessings on you. You have a very big heart.

RADHA: Thank you, Stella. It is probably the command of the Gods that I am blessed to do. Okay, what would you like to have?

Radha hands over the menu card. With curiosity, Stella browses the menu.

STELLA: Okay. I'll go for a veg burger and butterscotch ice cream. How about you?

RADHA: I had with the children. Since you got delayed, I decided to go with them.

STELLA: Due apologies, Radha. I just got stuck in the mad traffic.

Radha places an order with the waitress. Radha looks at Stella inquisitively.

RADHA: How is Mahesh?

STELLA: Professionally, he is doing good. A star performer in the country. He is likely to become the Vice President of Skincare Products.

RADHA: That's good to hear. Convey my congrats to him.

Stella slowly places her hands on Radha's hand.

STELLA (hesitantly): Radha, I feel I am the real culprit for your break-up.

RADHA (astounded): In what way?

STELLA: I cut into your family life.

RADHA (probingly): You cut into my life!

STELLA: Even after marrying you, Mahesh had an intimate affair with me. We continue to have.

RADHA: Oh! I'm not surprised by his extramarital affair. I guessed it earlier.

STELLA: We knew our actions were wrong, immoral, illegal, and unethical. Radha, we got stuck into it. The truth is we didn't know how to come out of it. We were in mad love.

RADHA: Both of you should have settled earlier if your love was that intense.

STELLA (tearfully): His parents objected to a Christian girl as their daughter-in-law. You know well that they are orthodox Brahmins. They told him they would leave the house if he married me. I even said to Mahesh that I would convert to

Hinduism if religion became the main factor coming as an impediment.

RADHA: Oh! That isn't good. Conversion for the sake of marriage is wrong.

STELLA: Mahesh didn't endorse the conversion aspect. He was dead against it. But, being the only son, Mahesh bowed to their pressure. Moreover, he had a defect in his horoscope. Getting a Brahmin girl was not easy with a Manglik dhosham. Somehow, you came into his life as your horoscope matched. He liked your profile. He discussed it with me. I encouraged him to look at you as his prospective life partner.

RADHA: I feel sad for both of you.

STELLA: When his parents objected to our relationship, he landed in partial depression. Because of his depression, he had mood swings. I thought of quitting the organisation two years ago. He pleaded with me not to leave him. Well, my presence made him overcome the depression.

RADHA: So sad! Your presence helped him a lot. No doubt. You did a great job in taking care of him.

STELLA: After he found you as a suitable match, I thought of quitting again, as I felt it was not correct to be with him anymore. I thought my presence would corrupt his mind. Once again, he pleaded that he would land into depression without me. He trapped me emotionally. I yielded to his request.

RADHA: Stella, to be candid, we didn't have a good romantic life. I love to have good sex. But I couldn't get one from Mahesh. Why blame him! Probably, I didn't know the way to satisfy him.

We were a mismatch on the bed. Good that you cared for his lustful desires to his satisfaction and delight. He needs it badly. Where will he go when he can't have good sex with his wife? I feel I'm the root cause of his extramarital affair. I need to take the blame myself to some extent.

STELLA: I had a feeling of marital discord between you people. Radha, I gave my body knowing his physical and mental condition. I didn't want him to land in a problem again. Circumstances forced me. Somehow, I didn't have the mind to leave him. I got emotionally attached to him.

RADHA: Had Mahesh talked about his affair, I wouldn't have come into his life. He made a big mistake entering marital life. I had this intuition that he has some soft corner for you. I am not surprised that both of you are having a good affair. You are his ideal partner in many ways.

STELLA: Radha, curse Mahesh and me in any way you want for what we have done to you. We deserve it. We need to take the punishment for our wrongdoings. Today, I decided to open it with you, come what may. I couldn't hold it inside my brain. I wanted to be at least open with you, if not faithful to you.

Radha places her right hand gently on Stella's hand.

RADHA: Cool, Stella. Don't be stupid with your words. I think God broke my relationship with Mahesh only to ensure that you come into his life as his life partner. Well, the same God had a different plan for me.

STELLA: I doubt if I would settle with him. We will continue to be intimate, but not as his wife. His parents will not accept me.

RADHA: You have faith in God! Humm!

STELLA: Yes.

RADHA: Stella, you'll unite with Mahesh. Mark my word, you'll be his wife soon.

STELLA: I doubt, Radha.

RADHA: I'll make it happen. Now God has given me another job to unite both of you. Trust me; I'll be successful in my endeavour.

The waitress places the burger and ice cream.

RADHA: Dear, have. Cheer up. I'll go to the play area and see the kids. I am taking them to the Guindy Zoological Park and the Planetarium.

STELLA: Oh! That's good. They will thoroughly enjoy it.

With Stella opening out about her life with Mahesh concisely, Radha feels there is no point in probing further. She has received enough information. Being a pragmatic and cheerful lady with noble intent, she now thinks she has to help Stella unite with Mahesh. Stella was brutally honest with her and admitted many facts openly. This act made Radha closer to her.

SCENE 62: INTERIOR, RIVER VIEW APARTMENT, RADHA'S FLAT, BEDROOM – EVENING

AFTER A WEEK – SATURDAY, 10:45 pm

Radha, dressed in her light rose colour nightie and resting on the bed, is watching the late evening music reality show. She seems to enjoy the melodious musical rendition by a Bengali female contestant singing the evergreen Lata Mangeshkar's hit song **'Solah Baras Ki Bali Umar'** *from the superhit Hindi film* **Ek Dujje Ke Liye.** *Her mobile phone rings. She picks it up and, to her surprise, notices the caller. Lowering the volume of the TV,*

RADHA: Hi Mahesh!

Intercut with Mahesh, who is resting on the couch and seeing the T 20 cricket match.

MAHESH: Hi Radha! Good evening. Did I disturb you?

RADHA: No, no. I am watching the music reality show. Your call surprised me. Anyway, how are you and your parents?

MAHESH: Everyone is doing good, thank you. Stella told me that she had met you. First of all, congrats and good wishes for your stupendous charitable work. My parents were in awe when I told them of your adoption of the two kids. Mark my words, Radha; my parents were in tears. They were visibly moved. Your noble act has opened their minds differently. You know, their perceptions of life have changed dramatically. So, I need to thank you for bringing that change.

RADHA: Oh! Thank you, Mahesh. I need to move on with life. Now that we have split, I think you should settle with your sweetheart, Stella. She is a beautiful lady. She did phenomenal work in your life. I feel both of you would make a good couple.

MAHESH (remorsefully & softly): I'm sorry, Radha, for what happened between us. I tender my unconditional apology to you for my mistakes. I should have opened up about my affair with you. Both Stella and I feel that we have done gross injustice to you. Radha, Stella was right in her statement. We deserve some punishment for our actions and wrong deeds.

RADHA: Forget it, Mahesh; the mistake is on my part too. Don't regret the past. Look for a bright future. Because of our breakup, I could take the two sweet kids and their grandmother with me. But, you know, many things in our lives are predetermined by the supreme forces above. It is our destiny.

MAHESH: To be honest, Radha, I am alive and kicking today because of Stella. She was my pillar of strength when I went through troubled times.

RADHA: I'm aware, Mahesh. She did tell me. What I liked about is her honesty. She is an ideal partner for you. Now, your parents will agree to your proposal. I'll come and convince your parents.

MAHESH: Radha, you are most welcome to my house any time. Just because we have split, our relationship doesn't end. My parents keep talking very high about you.

RADHA: By the way, Mahesh, we need to file our papers in the family court immediately to expedite our mutual consent divorce decree. Better to get it fast so that you can marry Stella. Instead of a divorce, I can seek to annul the marriage by telling the court that you were in a relationship with Stella earlier. Well, our lawyers can work out the best option.

MAHESH: Thanks, Radha, for the gesture. Appreciate it. What about your life?

RADHA: My life is with my two kids and their grandmother. My objective is to make them shine brilliantly in their lives. I want to show them a new world. So, I will help them in every way possible.

MAHESH (flabbergasted): Brilliant thought! But I think you should have a person in your life. You deserve one to enjoy many things. You are an extraordinary person.

RADHA: True. I'm a human being with all senses. I may go in for a live-in or partnership relationship if I desire. But no to marriage for few years because of obvious reasons. My mind is firm on that unless it changes dramatically one day to accept the institution of marriage again. Marriage is good and divine, but it has to work. I am tired of listening to horoscope dhosham and its consequences. Now, I have another hefty tag attached to my name – divorcee! To hell with all these things. I hate people talking at my back.

MAHESH: Radha, any help you want any time, call Stella and me. You can count on us. You'll always be in my prayers.

RADHA: Thank you so much, Mahesh. We will catch up later. Convey my regards to your parents. Tell them that one day I will drop in.

MAHESH: Most welcome. Cheers and good night.

CHAPTER 17

SCENE 63: EXTERIOR, INDIRA NAGAR, ADYAR – MORNING

After a month

Looking stylish with her coolers, Radha is driving her SUV smoothly on one of the interior avenue roads of the famous Indira Nagar of the Adyar area in Chennai. Daphne is seated beside her, and the two cute children, Vincent and Melinda, enjoy seeing the broad avenues. Radha elegantly stops in front of a modern independent double-storeyed house. Inside the compound, a puffy golden Labrador comes near the gate and barks a few times. Vincent and Melinda look excited, seeing the well-built canine. Hearing the bark, Kishore comes smilingly from the house towards the gate. He looks at his pet and pats him.

KISHORE: Oscar! Keep quiet. Go there.

Listening to the master, Oscar wags his tail impatiently. Finally, he stops barking but is keen to meet and greet the visitors. Blissfully, Kishore sees his guest.

KISHORE: Radha, welcome to my house. So lovely to see you all.

Oscar looks eager and charged, putting his forelegs on the gate. Looking at Oscar, Vincent and Melinda look enthusiastic and curious. Kishore opens the gate.

KISHORE: Oscar is keen to meet you all. He is highly playful. Your children will enjoy him.

When the guests enter the driveway, Oscar excitedly goes around them a few times and sniffs. He has got their identity now. Vincent and Melinda rub Oscar gently, and he seems to enjoy the warmth and affection shown by the young guests. Daphne is looking cautious and silent. Radha looks at Vincent and Melinda.

KISHORE: Both of you like Oscar!

VINCENT: Oscar looks too good, uncle.

RADHA: Kishore, it looks like my children have become close to Oscar. They are enjoying him. See the bonding! They are not afraid at all.

KISHORE: Oh! Oscar is too good at making friends. He loves good company. He will not leave them. Come.

Oscar leads the guest in the driveway towards the house. Kishore's new steel grey Mahindra Scorpio SUV is impressively parked at the end of the portico.

Kishore's mother, Vaidhehi, holding a circular plate, comes out of the house into the entrance. Kishore's father, Subramaniam, is standing just behind his wife. Joyfully, Vaidhehi sees Radha and other guests.

VAIDHEHI: Radha, wait. I'll take aarthi for you people. Look, you have come as a family for the first time into this house. The children look so cute.

RADHA: Aunty, why all these formalities?

VAIDHEHI: Please, ma. It is my desire. I'm like your mother.

RADHA: Okay, aunty.

Vaidhehi looks at the other members.

VAIDHEHI: Please, all of you, come closer to Radha.

As requested, Daphne stands next to Radha. The two kids are in front of her obediently. Radha gently places her hands on their shoulders. Vaidhehi shows the plate containing the sacred red kumkum water in front of them by gyrating her hands in a clockwise direction. Oscar is watching inquisitively the action taking place. Is he sensing something strange that he has not seen all these days? We know dogs have unique sensory perceptions. Kishore is mystified, looking at his mother performing this traditional act of welcoming guests. In a way, he is happy. This act is typically done only on specific occasions. Through the action, is Vaidhehi conveying any subtle and vital message? At one point, she impeded the unity of Kishore and Radha. Being a traditional lady, she didn't want Kishore to settle with Radha due to her severe Manglik defect in her horoscope. Vaidhehi looks at Radha.

VAIDHEHI: Radha, please come.

SCENE 64: INTERIOR, KISHORE'S HOUSE, LIVING ROOM – MORNING

Kishore ushers the guests into the main living hall. Oscar joins them jubilantly. All of them take a seat on the broad couch. Oscar sits on the floor close to Vincent and Melinda. Both keep rubbing him. Kishore is seated next to them. Vaidhehi goes near Radha ecstatically.

VAIDHEHI: Radha, come. I want to hug you. So happy to see you do wonderful things in life. You are a role model to us. Take my words; you will scale great heights in your professional and personal life.

Radha gets up, and she gently hugs Vaidhehi.

RADHA: Thank you so much, aunty, for your love and affection.

VAIDHEHI: So nice to see the two kids attached to you.

RADHA: I've been moving close with them for some time. Both are very intelligent. They like Kishore a lot.

VAIDHEHI: Radha, I have made special lunch. If children want, they can have it now.

RADHA: We can have it after one hour. We had a good breakfast.

Radha looks at Kishore.

RADHA: Kishore, if you don't mind, can you put some comic videos for them.

KISHORE: Sure.

Kishore looks at the two kids.

KISHORE: Shall I put Aladdin, The Little Mermaid or Kung Fu Panda? What do you want to see?

VINCENT (enthusiastically): Uncle, we will see Aladdin.

Vaidhehi goes near Radha and, in slow decibel, whispers.

VAIDHEHI: Radha, if you don't mind, why don't you come inside. I want to talk with you.

RADHA: Sure.

Vaidhehi ushers Radha into her bedroom. Kishore and his father look clueless. Daphne is watching the fascinating video along with her grandchildren.

SCENE 65: INTERIOR, KISHORE'S HOUSE, BEDROOM – MORNING

Radha is sitting casually on the queen size bed and looking curious as to why Vaidhehi wants to have a personal chat with her. Vaidhehi is closing the window curtains and switching on the AC. She comes and sits near Radha. Holding her hand, Vaidhehi looks at Radha softly.

VAIDHEHI: Radha, to be honest, I am seeing some form of God through you. What you have done is something remarkable. You have exhibited unbelievable maturity and thoughts.

RADHA: Aunty, please don't use big words. I'm a simple person. Whatever work I am doing is due to the grace of God.

VAIDHEHI: Radha, I know you must be angry with me that I cut into your life. I didn't allow Kishore to settle with you.

RADHA: That's okay, aunty. Your family believed in horoscope matching. I don't blame you at all. Why should I? The curse is on me that I am born with a horoscope defect.

VAIDHEHI: Radha, I am a changed person now. Why don't you marry Kishore? Humm! It is my humble request. Please. I am not bothered about the horoscope matching now. When God is inside you, why should I bother?

Radha places her hand on Vaidhehi's lap.

RADHA (a bit annoyed): Aunty, humble request. Please don't use the word horoscope again for marriage. I'm dead against it. The sound of that word makes me sick. Please don't mistake me, aunty; I'm not interested in marriage for a few more years. Another wedding will give me more headaches in many ways.

VAIDHEHI: When I can be flexible, why not you?

RADHA: If Kishore has some health issues at a later date, your subconscious mind will tell you that your son has married a Manglik dhosham person. Aunty, your mind cannot be away from it in your thoughts. Your relatives will taunt you if they come to know. Why all these headaches?

VAIDHEHI: Are you serious that you don't want to settle?

RADHA: Aunty. I have a family now to look after. That's my top primary priority. So, their happiness is my happiness. Marriage is secondary to me. I've discussed with Kishore on this.

VAIDHEHI (stunned): Are you going to be single in your life? It would be best if you had a partner to share many things with him.

RADHA: Aunty, I don't mind having a live-in relationship with Kishore if it is okay with him. I now feel comfortable with this kind of relationship rather than entering into marriage. My mind is clear on this. No ambiguity.

VAIDHEHI: Is Kishore okay with your proposal.

RADHA: I've given him time to think. No hurry at all. Kishore should feel comfortable with my family. It will be a new life for him too. If he wants, he can even look at any female to settle. It is fine with me. Aunty, I will not cut into his life. He needs a partner.

VAIDHEHI: Kishore is mad after you. He cannot think of any other female other than you in his life.

RADHA: Aunty, we like each other to the core. But circumstances have changed dramatically now. In another three months, we will be shifting to Singapore. We have decided to stay together in a big four-bedroom flat. So, let's see how our relationship goes. I know we will indeed have a good life with peace and happiness. But, through God's grace, if we are destined, it will lead to marriage at a later stage.

VAIDHEHI: Radha, my only prayer is that you and Kishore should be together. I can understand your feelings. You have a valid point. What I admire about you is your openness and clarity of thoughts. God bless you, dear. Come, we will go to the hall. All of them will be curious about our discussion here.

As Radha gets up, Vaidhehi gently hugs and kisses her on her cheek. Then, both of them walk into the hall. Vaidhehi has a glimmer of hope that Radha is not opposed to marriage, and she will unite with Kishore as a married couple one day. But the big question is – when? Due to some reason, if it doesn't happen, will Kishore leave Radha for good and look out for another female? We can only hope for something positive to turn out in their lives.

SCENE 66: INTERIOR, KISHORE'S HOUSE, LIVING ROOM – AFTERNOON

Looking at Radha and his mother, Kishore has a hunch that his mother has convinced Radha to settle with him. Kishore is keen to marry her, but Radha is not yielding to the proposal. Her past experiences are haunting her badly. With new dynamics emerging in her family life, Radha feels marrying Kishore could spell new issues at a later stage. His interests in her adopted family may not be there and could lead to disharmony. The best option she feels is to have a live-in relationship. It is 12:30 pm. Radha looks at the kids, who are eagerly watching the television.

RADHA: Sweeties, enjoying the TV? Humm!

The children nod their heads, affirming their happiness in watching the video. Vincent gets up and holds Radha's hands.

VINCENT: Aunty, this Kishore uncle will also be coming to Singapore with us?

RADHA: You ask him.

Vincent holds Kishore's hands.

VINCENT: Uncle, will you come with us. We want you.

KISHORE: I am coming, dear. I'll stay at your house only. Okay!

VINCENT: How about Oscar?

KISHORE (smilingly): I'll get one Oscar for you there. Happy!

Vincent offers a high five to Kishore. Vaidhehi feels elated listening to Kishore. However, she still hopes that Radha will yield to settling down with her son one day.

VAIDHEHI: Kishore, put banana leaves on the dining table. I'll bring the food. Let them have lunch.

Having food on banana leaves is considered auspicious and sacred in Hindu custom.

DAPHNE: Madam, I'll help you organise the food on the table. I'll take care of the kids. Don't worry.

SCENE 67: EXTERIOR, ANNA INTERNATIONAL AIRPORT TERMINAL, CHENNAI – MORNING.

16th August, 2019

The sprawling departure terminal is buzzing with plenty of activities. Undoubtedly, the airport has become significantly busy with many connections to numerous international destinations. Chennai has seen tremendous growth in various industrial sectors in the last two decades. The city has acquired a unique tag of being the **Detroit of Asia**, *with major automobile giants having factories in and around the city. As a result, Chennai has earned the unique distinction as the Gateway to South India.*

Mahesh, Stella, and Mahesh's parents eagerly look toward the vehicles coming and stopping. Stella, wearing a traditional burgundy silk saree, is enticingly beautiful. Small Jasmine garland pinned to her curly tresses behind enhances her attractiveness. Slowly two white Toyota Innova vehicles halt in front of them. Charm and grace personified, Radha comes out with Daphne, Vincent and Melinda. Radha is in her typical semi-formal attire of ankle-length white cotton pants with a bluish-black linen blouse. Smartly dressed in vibrant colours, the two kids look exuberant to have their maiden flight journey to Singapore. Behind their vehicle emerge Radha's mother and her maternal aunty. Radha is stunned to see Mahesh's parents. She never expected them to come for the send-off. Gracefully and symbolically, she goes near them and bends to touch their feet to seek their blessings. Moorthy and Lalitha place their hands on her head to bless her traditionally. Lalitha, with tears rolling, hugs Radha.

LALITHA: Radha, our blessings are always with you. Thank you so much for all the help rendered to my family. We thank you for uniting Mahesh with Stella. I think you played a significant role in convincing us. You changed our attitude and behaviour. You showed us what humanity is all about.

RADHA: Amma, everything happened for good. It is the grace of God. My love and affection will always be there for you people.

Lalitha takes the small box from her shoulder bag. She opens it and takes a diamond-studded bracelet.

LALITHA: Radha, show your right hand.

RADHA: Amma, why all these formalities?

LALITHA: This gift is a small token of our love and affection.

Lalitha gently ties the bracelet to Radha's hand.

RADHA: Amma, thank you so much.

Radha's mother comes forward and offers her respects to Mahesh's parents. From a short distance, Mahesh and Stella, with happiness radiating, slowly approaches, pushing the empty trolleys. They gently come and hug Radha. Stella gives her sweet kisses to Vincent and Melinda. Radha looks at Stella.

RADHA: Stella, with jasmine flowers and saree, you look like a typical beautiful Tamil brahmin girl.

She looks at Mahesh.

RADHA (sarcastically): What, Mahesh! Stella is looking more gorgeous than your ex. Perfect match for you in many ways. She knows how to carry on with you!

MAHESH (smilingly): Radha, enough! Don't pull words from my mouth.

RADHA: When do you expect the divorce decree to come from the Court?

MAHESH: The lawyer told me within two months.

RADHA: Fair enough. Any help from my side, you can connect with my advocate. Please let me know if you need my presence before the Court.

MAHESH: Sure.

RADHA (enthusiastically): Mahesh, I'm sponsoring your honeymoon trip to Singapore as a token of love and affection to both of you.

MAHESH: Thank you so much. Appreciate your offer.

RADHA: I'll also join you people with my partner, Kishore. We all can go to Phuket for a week.

STELLA (excited): Cool, Radha. Sounds great!

Radha has again reiterated that she will have a partnership relationship with Kishore. Somehow, her mind is sturdy on this aspect and not willing to be flexible. But, with time, will her mind change? Only God can answer this question.

RADHA: Mahesh, if you don't mind, can I have one more trolley for Kishore. He will arrive any moment.

MAHESH: Sure, I'll get it.

RADHA: Thank you, dear.

Mahesh's parents are having a casual and harmonious discussion with Radha's mother, Seetha, despite the family separation. Both families have reconciled to bury the differences and looking forward to a bright future. Slowly, Kishore's Mahindra Scorpio SUV approaches and gently stops near them. He comes out delightfully wearing blue jeans, a matching T-shirt, and an open jacket. His parents, Subramanian and Vaidhehi, stand near him. Mahesh hugs Kishore gracefully.

MAHESH: Kishore, shall I help you keep your suitcases on the trolley?

KISHORE: Oh! Thank you, Mahesh.

Mahesh keeps the two cases on the trolley. Kishore puts the cabin baggage on top of them. Radha slowly comes and offers her respects to Kishore's parents by bending down and touching their feet to seek their blessings.

VAIDHEHI: God will shower enormous blessings on you.

Stella shakes hands with Kishore. From a short distance, Sr.Angela and Sr.Jennifer are approaching them. Radha spots them and receives them ecstatically. They hug Radha. Radha, in a customary way, bends down to touch their feet to seek their blessings. The sisters place their hands on Radha's head.

Sr.ANGELA: Radha, the Lord, will do many good things for you. We will miss you, dear.

RADHA: Sister, I am emotionally touched by both of you coming to the airport. Your good wishes and blessings are always there for me.

Seeing them, Daphne, Vincent and Melinda smilingly come and hug the sisters. Sr.Angela sees the two kids cheerfully.

Sr.ANGELA: Vincent, Melinda, here.

She gives them a Cadbury Five-Star chocolate bar. The kids happily receive them.

*It is time for Radha, her new family members, and Kishore to depart. For one last time, they shake hands and hug the visitors. They are embarking on a new journey in their lives to **a new world and a new horizon.** They bid adieu with renewed hopes and aspirations and proceed towards the main departure concourse area.*